☆ TEACHING ☆ AMERICAN HISTORY WITH ART MASTERPIECES

by Bobbi Chertok, Goody Hirshfeld, and Marilyn Rosh

SCHOLASTIC
PROFESSIONAL BOOKS

New York ☆ Toronto ☆ London ☆ Auckland ☆ Sydney

DEDICATED TO OUR OTHER PARTNERS:
Neal, Harvey, and Mel

ACKNOWLEDGMENTS

The authors wish to thank Harry Kels Swan of the Swan Historical Foundation; Jeffrey Dosik of the National Park Service, Ellis Island National Monument; and Kenyon B. FitzGerald, Jr., president of the Seventh Regiment Fund. We also appreciate the additional information provided by Karen Rinaldo, the artist of *The First Thanksgiving*; Sylvia Sprigg of Rokeby; the Marblehead Historical Society; and the Plimouth Plantation. Special appreciation is given to Richard Piatelli, Adult Services Librarian at the Nanuet Public Library.

Cover design by Vincent Ceci and Jaime Lucero

Interior design by Ellen Matlach Hassell
for Boultinghouse & Boultinghouse, Inc.

Interior illustration by Delana Bettoli and Manuel Rivera

ISBN 0-590-96402-X

About Living Art Seminars

In 1973 Bobbi Chertok, Goody Hirshfeld, and Marilyn Rosh created Living Art Seminars, a nonprofit organization designed to bring fine art into the classroom through a variety of programs. Its goal is to make art fresh, fun, and relevant to each and every child. Thousands of elementary schoolchildren and their teachers have awakened to a new appreciation of art through Living Art Seminars. As part of this program, students and teachers also visit museums, where they discover the excitement and beauty of art. Students learn respect for and understanding of different cultures. The seminars stimulate critical thinking with emphasis on observing, sequencing, listening, and reasoning. As a writer for the *New York Times* has observed, "With the help of Living Art Seminars, students are discovering that art is a lot closer and more fun than they had imagined." Over the years, Living Art Seminars has received numerous state and local grants.

In 1992 the founders of Living Art Seminars captured some of their time-tested techniques in *Meet the Masterpieces: Strategies, Activities, and Posters to Explore Great Works of Art.* Published the following year, *Meet the Masterpieces: Learning About Ancient Civilizations Through Art* focused on eight ancient cultures. *Month-by-Month Masterpieces*, published in 1996 highlights ten significant works of art, one for each month of the school year. All are published by Scholastic.

Contents

Introduction
The Purpose of This Book 6
How to Use This Book 7
Suggestions for Culminating Activities 9

The First Thanksgiving/1621 by Karen Rinaldo
USA Yesterday 10
The Picture Tells a Story 12
A Voice from the Picture 16
HANDS-ON STUDENT PAGES
Packing Advisory 17
Selling the New World 18
Extension Activities 19

Midnight Ride of Paul Revere by Grant Wood
USA Yesterday 20
The Picture Tells a Story 22
A Voice from the Picture 24
HANDS-ON STUDENT PAGES
Business Cards 25
The British Are Coming! 26
Extension Activities 27

Washington Crossing the Delaware by Emanuel Gottlieb Leutze
USA Yesterday 28
The Picture Tells a Story 30
A Voice from the Picture 33
HANDS-ON STUDENT PAGES
George vs. George 34
Dialogue 35
Extension Activities 36

The Trail of Tears by Robert Lindneux
USA Yesterday 37
The Picture Tells a Story 39
A Voice from the Picture 41
HANDS-ON STUDENT PAGES
Map Study 42
Original Poetry 43
Extension Activities 44

Forward by Jacob Lawrence
   USA Yesterday 45
   The Picture Tells a Story 47
   A Voice from the Picture 50
   HANDS-ON STUDENT PAGES
      Stitching a Path to Freedom 51
      Stamp of Approval 52
   Extension Activities 53

Departure of the Seventh Regiment for the War, April 19, 1861
by Thomas Nast
   USA Yesterday 54
   The Picture Tells a Story 56
   A Voice from the Picture 58
   HANDS-ON STUDENT PAGES
      Reading a Map 59
      Political Cartoons: Pictures with Punch 60
   Extension Activities 61

Across the Continent. "Westward the Course of Empire Takes Its Way"
by James Merritt Ives and Fanny Palmer
   USA Yesterday 62
   The Picture Tells a Story 64
   A Voice from the Picture 67
   HANDS-ON STUDENT PAGES
      Wheels West 68
      The Well-Dressed Cowboy 69
   Extension Activities 70

Welcome to New York City from *Frank Leslie's Illustrated Newspaper*
   USA Yesterday 71
   The Picture Tells a Story 73
   A Voice from the Picture 75
   HANDS-ON STUDENT PAGES
      Advice Column 76
      Immigrants: Then and Now .77
   Extension Activities 78

Answers 79

The Purpose of This Book

You and your students are about to start a journey through America's past. The major goal of this journey is to shake the cobwebs off history by presenting it in a way that is both entertaining and informative—through art.

The eight works of art in this book deal with events that span this country's history from 1621 to the late nineteenth century. They show an untamed wilderness growing into villages, towns, and major cities. They depict journeys, celebrations, and acts of courage.

In studying the art, you and your students will enter the lives of people from America's past. In the process you will learn not only about them but also about yourselves. It is our hope that as you visit with the individuals who helped build this country, your class will respect and appreciate their unique differences.

The featured works of art include:

(Dates in parentheses denote the year the historical event took place.)

⭐ ***The First Thanksgiving/1621*** by Karen Rinaldo, painted in 1995

This painting celebrates the interaction between two American cultures—the Wampanoag Indians and the European settlers—as they discover that giving thanks is common to both their traditions.

⭐ ***Midnight Ride of Paul Revere*** (1775) by Grant Wood, painted in 1931

Paul Revere's warning to the colonists is magically illuminated in this painting as the patriots prepare at a moment's notice to fight for freedom.

⭐ ***Washington Crossing the Delaware*** (1776) by Emanuel Gottlieb Leutze, completed in 1851

In this painting, Washington's sheer personal magnetism and the genius of his strategy turn a near-defeated army to victory.

⭐ ***The Trail of Tears*** (1830s) by Robert Lindneux, painted in 1942

The Cherokee people are portrayed as they are forced to embark upon their journey of removal from their homes in the South to a strange and inhospitable territory in the West.

⭐ ***Forward*** (1857) by Jacob Lawrence, painted in 1967

Harriet Tubman is portrayed here as a heroine who put aside all thoughts of personal safety in order to free her people.

⭐ *Departure of the Seventh Regiment for the War, April 19, 1861*
by Thomas Nast, painted in 1869

Patriotic Americans are portrayed cheering the Seventh Regiment as it marches off to defend Washington City. The confederate army had successfully captured Fort Sumter, the act that began the American Civil War.

⭐ *Across the Continent. "Westward the Course of Empire Takes Its Way"*
(1868), published the same year by the printing firm of Currier and Ives

This print celebrates the energetic growth of America as the railroad connects the East to the West. At the same time it alerts us to the plight of the newly displaced Native Americans and the impact of industrialization on our natural environment.

⭐ *Welcome to New York City* (1887) by an unknown artist, published in an illustrated newspaper on July 2 of the same year

European immigrants are shown passing by the Statue of Liberty as they seek freedom and the promise of a better life in America.

How to Use This Book

This book is divided into eight sections, each focusing on one piece of art and the particular event in history that it depicts. Each section consists of five parts.

USA Yesterday

This two-page reproducible newspaper introduces each work of art. It presents the events that occurred before the moment shown in the art so that students will become familiar with the atmosphere of the time, meet well-known people of the period, and learn about their lives. The news stories and features (editorials, weather reports, sports reports, classified ads, games, and announcements) have been adapted from actual historical accounts or reports in newspapers. Answers to the games and quizzes appear in the back of the book.

Read the newspaper aloud with students. Encourage questions and comparisons with the news today. If students have visited historic sites relevant to the period under discussion, ask if they or their families can bring in pictures or artifacts. Ask the school librarian to set aside books pertaining to the time.

The Picture Tells a Story

This section is a teacher's guide in the form of a question-and-answer dialogue about the work of art. The questions are designed to encourage students to observe, imagine, articulate ideas, express feelings, and use critical-thinking skills. Many questions are open-ended and may lead to surprising detours as students share their own interpretations of the artists' work. Some questions have more specific answers that students can find in their issues of *USA Yesterday*, while others may serve as springboards for additional research.

Each question-and-answer section includes a short comment about the artist or the circumstances surrounding the release of the artwork. Students may want to do further research on the artist and look for additional works by him or her. They can also extend their learning by identifying works by different artists that depict the same event. Encourage students to observe similarities and differences in artists' interpretations.

A Voice from the Picture

Imagine that the artwork has come to life and that one person has stepped out of the picture to share his or her story. You may read this first-person account to students and invite them to guess which character in the work is speaking. The Discussion Question at the conclusion of the feature prompts students to relate further to the painting.

Invite students to bring another individual from the art to life by creating for him or her an extemporaneous speech, a dialogue, or even a drama.

Hands-on Student Pages

These reproducible pages encourage students to connect the ideas in the artwork to their own world either in writing or through art of their own. When you distribute an activity page, review the directions with the class and encourage students to respond creatively.

Extension Activities

This section includes a variety of additional activities for you to select from to build students' critical-thinking skills and to extend the learning experience across the curriculum.

Many of the activities require student research. Students may search for materials in libraries, at historic societies, and on the Internet. You may want to assign different activities to different students depending on their individual strengths and interests. Some activities can be done alone, while some lend themselves to cooperative learning. Answers for some extension activities are included in the answer section at the back of the book.

Suggestions for Culminating Activities

You may want to try some of the following activities to help students reinforce or synthesize what they've learned while studying these works of art.

1 Ask students to explain how two or more of the works of art express a similar idea in different ways.

EXAMPLES

- The Pilgrims in *The First Thanksgiving/1621* and the settlers going west in *Across the Continent* have both embarked on exciting, dangerous journeys although for different reasons.
- The Cherokee people in *The Trail of Tears* and the immigrants in *Welcome to New York City* are both on journeys, but the circumstances of the journeys vary.
- Three of the paintings—*Midnight Ride of Paul Revere, Washington Crossing the Delaware,* and *Forward*—feature a forceful individual who made a difference in American history.
- *Washington Crossing the Delaware* and *Departure of the Seventh Regiment for the War* are both about Americans engaged in war.

2 Using the "issues" of *USA Yesterday* as models, students can publish a class newspaper about the important historical events under study.

3 Students might like to present one or more of the historical events in another way.

EXAMPLES

- Students can write and perform stories, plays, or poems about these exciting moments in history.
- Students can work together to create their own original works of art—dioramas, murals, or collages—depicting the historical events.

4 Your class may like to stage a reenactment of one or more of the historical events explored in this book. They may also want to set aside an entire day to dress in costume, eat the foods, and play the games of that time period.

THE JOURNEY BEGINS

SEPTEMBER 6, 1620 — The ship *Mayflower* set sail for the New World today with 102 persons aboard. At least 35 of the passengers are the Separatists, also known as Pilgrims. They are leaving England in search of religious freedom. They hope to find a place where they can worship God in their own way. Also on board are people who do not share the Pilgrims' beliefs. The Pilgrims refer to them as Strangers. They are adventurers who hope to find their fortune in the New World.

TROUBLES AT SEA

OCTOBER 1620 — A frightening and dangerous event took place at sea during a terrible storm. A huge wave smashed into the *Mayflower* and cracked the main beam that supported the deck and braced the sides of the ship. Wood splintered. Water flooded through the roof of the lower deck and onto the terrified Pilgrims. They thought the end was near. Fortunately, a heavy metal screw was found, and it was used to hold the beam in place. Captain Christopher Jones announced to the passengers that the *Mayflower* was badly damaged but that disaster had been averted.

Medical Updates, 1620

- A bandage of cooked onions can cure the bite of a mad dog.
- Bathing more than once a month is bad for one's health.

leech: worm used to suck blood from sick people

mortar and pestle: tool used to grind herbs

Birth Announcements

OCTOBER 16, 1620 — Mr. and Mrs. Steven Hopkins proudly announce the birth of their son, Oceanus, while at sea aboard the *Mayflower*. Another son, Giles, and two daughters, Constance and Damaris, complete the happy family.

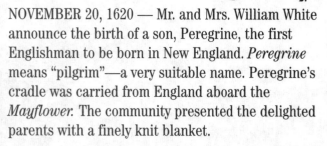

NOVEMBER 20, 1620 — Mr. and Mrs. William White announce the birth of a son, Peregrine, the first Englishman to be born in New England. *Peregrine* means "pilgrim"—a very suitable name. Peregrine's cradle was carried from England aboard the *Mayflower*. The community presented the delighted parents with a finely knit blanket.

ARRIVAL: HARD TIMES

FEBRUARY 1621 — The Pilgrims finally spotted land around November 9, 1620. However, hard choices still awaited them. It was difficult to agree on a place to settle. The first stop, Cape Cod, was a barren, gray, and uninviting area. The Pilgrims explored many sites before finally deciding on their future home. The most welcoming location seemed to be a village deserted by Patuxet natives. The Pilgrims named their home in the New World, New Plymouth.

During this winter of 1620–1621, the Pilgrims have been suffering great despair because of the cold weather and lack of food. More than half of the original voyagers have died.

SQUANTO TO THE RESCUE

MARCH 22, 1621 — At just the right moment, a Native American named Squanto walked out of the forest and offered his help to the sick and weakened Pilgrims. It is he who has taught the newcomers how to survive.

Squanto is a survivor himself. Many years ago, he had been taken from his village and brought to England, where he learned to speak the Pilgrims' language. When he returned to his native shores, he found that his entire tribe, the Patuxet, had been wiped out by a deadly plague. He was alone in the world—the only living Patuxet brave left.

Squanto offered his help to the struggling community of Pilgrims. In April, he showed the Pilgrims the streams where thousands of herring could be caught for fertilizing the crops. With Squanto at their side, the Pilgrims learned to plant corn, hunt, and fish. The English settlers recognized their debt to Squanto and treated him with love and respect.

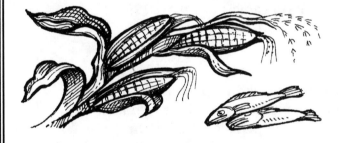

Game: Pilgrims Pack a Snack

Patience and Charity, two young women of Plymouth, regularly pack a basket of food to give to a neighbor. What will future generations of Americans call these foods? Write the number of the food listed in Column A next to its twenty-first-century equivalent in Column B.

Column A	Column B
1. hardtack	___ pumpkins
2. johnnycake	___ blueberries
3. pompions	___ spinach
4. cow cumber pickles	___ stew
5. whortle-berries	___ cucumbers
6. spinage	___ cornmeal cake
7. pottage	___ flour biscuit

PEACE TREATY SIGNED

MARCH 22, 1621 — After friendly entertainment and the exchange of some gifts, Wampanoag Sachem [chief] Massasoit signed a peace treaty with Edward Winslow of the Plymouth colony. The groups have pledged not to hurt or steal from each other and to leave their weapons behind when they visit. They also promise to assist each other if attacked.

MASSASOIT

EDWARD WINSLOW

WEDDING BELLS

JUNE 10, 1621 — The entire Plymouth congregation celebrated the wedding of Priscilla Mullins to Mr. John Alden, formerly a cooper [barrel maker] from Harwich, England. The bride wore a linen cap and a dark blue, wide-collared dress with deeply cut cuffs, which she brought over from England on the *Mayflower*. The groom wore a dark brown doublet [jacket], green knee breeches above tan stockings, and laced leather shoes. Priscilla is the only surviving member of her family. Her parents and young brother died in Plymouth, last winter.

Did You Know That...?

• Passenger William Mullins brought over on the *Mayflower* 126 pairs of shoes and 13 pairs of boots.

• Musical favorites in the New World are "The Lovesick Maid," "Love Overcomes All Things," and "The Two Faithful Lovers."

THE PICTURE TELLS A STORY
The First Thanksgiving/1621

DIMENSIONS: **36 in. x 60 in.**   MEDIUM: **oil on canvas**   DATE: **1995**

ABOUT THE ARTIST: *Karen Rinaldo*

Born in Worcester, Massachusetts, Karen Rinaldo has found a good part of her artistic inspiration in the history, color, and mood of Cape Cod. In 1994, Karen Rinaldo was commissioned by the National Association of Congregational Christian Churches to create a historically accurate painting of the first Thanksgiving. For six months, Rinaldo carefully researched this event in much the same way that an archaeologist attempts to reconstruct an ancient village. One year later, her painting, *The First Thanksgiving/1621*, was presented to Pilgrim Hall Museum, Plymouth, Massachusetts, where it hangs today.

⭐ *Questions for Class Discussion*

1 Who are the people in the painting?

The English Pilgrims and Strangers who traveled to America on the *Mayflower* are joined by their new friends, the Native Americans of the Wampanoag tribe.

2 Why have they gathered together?

The settlers want to give thanks for the abundant crops they were able to harvest. With enough food stored to last through the coming winter, the Pilgrims are confident that their colony will endure.

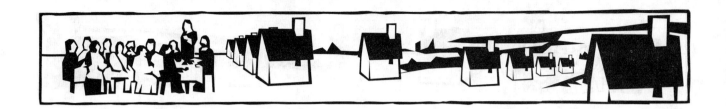

3 Why did the Pilgrims invite the Wampanoag to join them?

The Pilgrims knew that without the help of the Wampanoag, they would not have survived. More than half of the Pilgrims died during the first winter. Then, on March 16, 1621, a chief named Samoset walked into their struggling settlement. He was unarmed and astonished the settlers by knowing a bit of their language. A few days later, Samoset brought the remarkable Squanto to Plymouth. Squanto taught the Pilgrims how to live in the wilderness. He also introduced them to Massasoit, the chief of all the tribes in the area. Massasoit and the Pilgrims signed a peace treaty, which lasted fifty-four years.

4 Are any of the settlers or Wampanoag armed?

No. Part of the peace treaty provided that everyone would leave his weapons behind during visits. The settlers and the Wampanoag also agreed not to hurt or steal from each other and to come to each other's aid if attacked by outsiders.

5 What did Squanto teach the settlers about gathering and growing food in the new land?

Squanto taught them to plant Indian corn using herring, a fish, for fertilizer. He pointed out which wild fruits and berries were safe to eat. He demonstrated how to make traps to catch lobsters and cod in the water around Plymouth. Further, Squanto encouraged the Pilgrims to eat wild duck, turkey, and deer, which could be hunted in the nearby forests.

6 Which animals will be eaten at the Thanksgiving feast? Can you locate them?

Two women at the left are carrying a cooked turkey on a platter. To the right of center, you can see three deer in a pen. In front of them, a group of Wampanoag surround an outdoor grill called a spit. It is made of tree limbs that are tied on the top and support the meat, which hangs over the fire. The Wampanoag are probably cooking venison, which is deer meat. Venison was an important part of this Thanksgiving menu. To the right, a Wampanoag brave is bringing a duck to the feast.

7 What other animals can you find?

A spaniel and a mastiff dog, two pigs, and several sheep. The pilgrims brought these animals over on the *Mayflower*.

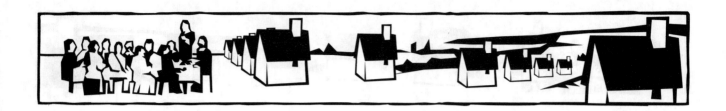

8 **Who do you think would get the honor of sitting at the head table (in the left foreground of the painting)?**

The most important men in both the Native American and settler communities are represented at the head table. Facing us is Squanto on the left, and next to him is Massasoit, wearing his bone necklace. Alongside Massasoit is Captain Miles Standish, the military protector of the colony. Next is John Alden, the carpenter and barrel maker, and Edward Winslow, who was responsible for the treaty with Massasoit. The elder of the church and the leader of the Pilgrims, William Brewster, stands and offers a prayer of thanksgiving. William Bradford, the governor of the colony, sits at the head of the table. To Bradford's left are the doctor Sam Fuller and his son, Sam, Jr. It was considered good manners for children to stand at the table while eating.

9 **On what kind of chairs are the guests sitting?**

Bradford and Brewster are seated in nicely carved chairs that they brought from England. The rest of the guests sit on benches, upended barrels, and stools—any object that could be used for seating. Massasoit was expected at the feast, but he surprised the Pilgrims by bringing along ninety Wampanoag braves. Not only was there a shortage of chairs, but the colonists had to build more tables and do some extra hunting and fishing to make sure there was enough to eat. The Wampanoag helped by bringing gifts of food. They all had a great deal to be thankful for. The party went on for three days.

10 **What materials were used to make the settlers' houses?**

Since the settlement was surrounded by forests, most houses were made from wood. The A-shaped roofs were thatched with sun-dried reeds. This design allowed the snow and rain to slide down the sides. The main room usually had a wooden floor and a large, stone fireplace for both cooking and heating the house. Do you notice the smoke curling out of several chimneys? The windows were covered with oiled paper or linen to let in some light.

11 **Why do you think the small house at the left of the painting is different from the others?**

This dark, damp house, which is partly underground, is called a hovel. The troublesome Billington family lived here, and you can see young Francis near the door. From the start of the voyage the Billingtons did not fit in with the other voyagers. Their language and their manners were very rough. The boys were mischievous—Francis almost blew up the *Mayflower* when he got his hands on some gunpowder, and John wandered off into the wilderness and a search party had to be formed to rescue him. Their father did not care for hard work, and while other men labored to build suitable houses, he was content to dig out a hovel for his family.

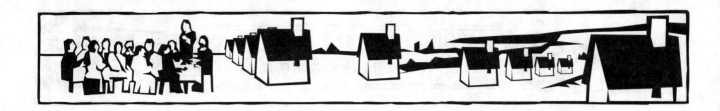

12 **What is the young woman in the center of the painting doing?**

Eighteen-year-old Priscilla Mullins seems to be talking with several of the younger children of the colony. Oceanus Hopkins, the baby born at sea, is in the cradle. Three little girls surround him: Humility Cooper in front, Resolved White, and Mary Allerton behind. The two sons of William Brewster, Wrastle and Love, are dressed for the occasion with white collars and knee-length pants.

13 **Where in the painting is Plymouth Rock? Where is the shallop (open boat) that carried the travelers to shore?**

The rock is on the left, in the top third of the painting. (Nobody knows whether the Pilgrims actually landed on this rock.) The shallop is floating between two land areas in the center of the painting.

A Wampanoag Brave Speaks

I have watched many seasons come and go. Spring is the time to clear and plant the fields. The long, warm days of summer are spent weeding our crops, digging for clams, and fishing. When fall comes, and the days are colder, it is time to hunt the deer and bear. My father taught me the rhythm of the seasons, and I will pass this knowledge on to my son.

One cold morning as I was out hunting, I saw a boat bigger than any I had seen before. I watched tired, sick men, women, and children struggle to shore. They did not look like anyone I had ever seen. I did not approach them.

Later, Massasoit, the great sachem, our chief, explained that they are strangers from far across the water. They know nothing of my land. They have come here not knowing when to plant the corn or how to catch the fish. My people believe in sharing with strangers when they are hungry. So we have taught the newcomers how to plant, and they survive. They want to thank us because they now have a good harvest. I am one of the braves chosen by Massasoit to help celebrate their good fortune. We bring along fowl and deer, which we cook together over an open fire.

I do not know what to think about these people who now live on our land.

*Discussion **Q**uestion* **What conclusion do you think the Wampanoag brave will eventually reach about the presence of the white settlers?**

Packing Advisory

The following list was published in England in 1618. Suppose you were traveling today to another planet. Your mission is to colonize the planet. Suppose, too, that the space agency is providing space suits and all the computer equipment the mission requires. However, you can bring along some personal items that will make life in this new environment comfortable. On the bottom of this page, using the categories specified, list the items you would take along.

WARNING! Many settlers have left for the NEW WORLD unprepared for the journey and their destination. We therefore publish the following list of necessary articles.

APPAREL (for one man)	**TOOLS** (for a family of 6)	**VICTUALS** (for 6)	**HOUSEHOLD GOODS**
3 shirts	2 broad axes	8 bushels of meale	1 iron pot
1 waiste coat	2 steel hand saws	2 bushels of pease	1 kettle
4 pairs of shoes	2 hammers	2 bushels oatmeale	1 large frying pan
1 rug for a bed (to be filled with straw)	2 spades	1 gallon of water	1 spit
	1 grindstone	1 gallon of oyle	platters and dishes
	nails of all sorts	2 gallons of vinegar	spoons of wood

APPAREL

1. _____
2. _____
3. _____
4. _____

FOODS

1. _____
2. _____
3. _____
4. _____

TOOLS

1. _____
2. _____
3. _____
4. _____

OTHER SUPPLIES

1. _____
2. _____
3. _____
4. _____

Selling the New World

While the Pilgrims came to the New World for religious freedom, other settlers came for financial gain. The following illustration and text come from a pamphlet advertising Virginia. The company running this ad has invested money in Virginia and now will pay people to go there and plant crops.

In the space at the bottom of the page, create an ad that will persuade adventurous people to leave their homes and start life over in a faraway place. You can advertise an existing place or create one of your own.

In an old form of English, the letter *f* sometimes represented the sound we show with *s*. So the words above the picture of the ship say, "Exciting all *such* as be well affected to further the *same*," which means something like, "Calling all persons who can do such planting."

NOVA BRITANNIA.
OFFERING MOST
Excellent fruites by Planting in
VIRGINIA.

Exciting all such as be well affected
to further the same.

LONDON
Printed for SAMVEL MACHAM, and are to be sold at
his Shop in Pauls Church-yard, at the
Signe of the Bul-head.
1609.

Corbis-Bettmann

✪ *Rules of the Game*

Pilgrim children played a variety of games. Most of their toys were handmade, including hoops and sticks, balls, marbles, tops, stilts, and shuttlecocks (pieces of cork or similar material with one rounded end and one flat end, in which feathers are stuck). Ask students to do individual or group research about such homemade toys. After they explain how these toys were used in colonial times, have them create an updated version of one of the Pilgrim games.

✪ *Mapmaking*

Many of the meetings between the Pilgrims and the Native Americans occurred on what is now Cape Cod and southeast Massachusetts. Direct students to use reference materials that will help them draw a map of this area. On their maps, they should locate

a. the harbor where the *Mayflower* first arrived (today's Provincetown Harbor)

b. Corn Hill, where the Pilgrims discovered buried corn and took it

c. First Encounter Beach (between today's Eastham and Wellfleet), where hostilities between the Pilgrims and Native Americans occurred

d. Plymouth, the name given to the Pilgrims' settlement

✪ *Conflict Resolution*

The Pilgrims and the Wampanoags had a number of differences that might have led to conflict had they not worked together to draft a peace treaty that lasted more than 50 years. Can you think of other conflicts either in American history or in your own life that might have been avoided or resolved if the people involved had worked together to draft a peace treaty or a compact? What might the treaty have said?

✪ *Feast Arithmetic*

Ask the class to imagine that they are in charge of organizing the food for the first Thanksgiving feast for 140 guests. Have them consider the following problems.

a. Each guest will be served deer, turkey, and duck. If a deer feeds fourteen people, a turkey feeds ten people, and a duck feeds seven people, how many deer, turkeys, and ducks are needed?

b. If it takes two ears of corn to make a corn patty, and each guest will be offered one patty, how many ears of corn will feed 140 guests?

c. If it takes one pint of berries to make a pie, and if each pie serves eight people, how many pints of berries must be picked?

RALLY, MOHAWKS!

BOSTON, DECEMBER 16, 1773 — Hundreds of onlookers saw Paul Revere in action at the Boston Tea Party. He and about 150 other patriots disguised themselves as Mohawk Indians and took part in a protest against unfair taxation on tea by the British. Using their axes and making wild whooping sounds, they split open the tea chests stored on a British ship in the harbor. Then they dumped the contents into the water.

Samuel Adams, John Hancock, and Joseph Warren—leading members of the patriot group known as the Sons of Liberty—were also spotted in the vicinity.

A song glorifying the event was heard in the streets and taverns of Boston:

Rally, Mohawks! Bring out your axes
And tell King George we'll pay no taxes
On his foreign tea;
Our Warren's there, and bold Revere
With hands to do and words to cheer
For liberty and laws.

COLONISTS TARRING AND FEATHERING THE TAX COLLECTOR

The following cartoon has appeared in the London newspapers.

SECRET MEETING PLACE

DECEMBER 1773 — The Green Dragon Tavern in Boston is rumored to be the site where the patriots planned the strategy for the Boston Tea Party.

SECRETS AND SPIES

MARCH 1775 — The British are spying on Americans to find out when the colonies will be so bold as to try to break away from British rule. Groups of British redcoats have been seen taking off their uniforms and pretending to be American farmers. Some British spies have discovered large stores of gunpowder and weapons hidden by the American colonists twenty-one miles from Boston in the village of Concord.

THE PEOPLE WANT TO KNOW

APRIL 15, 1775 — Where will the British attack the colonists who are planning to rebel against the power of England? Paul Revere has instructed a friend to place a signal in the North Church steeple: *one lantern if the redcoats come by land, two if they come by sea.*

FLASH!

TUESDAY, APRIL 18, 1775 — The British are attacking Concord! Paul Revere and fellow patriot William Dawes received orders last night, to warn the countryside that the British are coming.

CLOSE UP: A PORTRAIT OF PAUL REVERE

APRIL 20, 1775 — Inquiring minds want to know: Who is Paul Revere and what does he look like? Several Years ago, the most accomplished artist of New England, John Singleton Copley, painted Paul Revere in his occupation as silversmith. Sadly, Mr. Copley no longer resides in the American colonies. Realizing that war was approaching, the portraitist moved to England last year to show his support for King George.

Culver Pictures

NO TASTE FOR TEA

JANUARY 1774 — Many citizens of other colonies are rushing to support the people of Boston. Other towns have either destroyed their stores of tea or locked the tea up in warehouses where it rots. In North Carolina, a gathering of ladies signed a declaration not to drink tea again, or to wear English cloth. Benjamin Franklin stated that the violent destruction of the tea seems to have united the American colonists.

NEWS FROM ENGLAND, 1775

- Noted engineer James Watts has sold his first steam engine.
- The British Parliament has heard a speech begging the government to settle their differences with the American colonies.

OTHER NEWS FROM THE COLONIES

PHILADELPHIA, 1775 — The first American anti-slavery organization has been established by Benjamin Franklin and Dr. Benjamin Rush. It is called the Society for the Relief of Free Negroes Unlawfully Held in Bondage.

THE PICTURE TELLS A STORY
Midnight Ride of Paul Revere

DIMENSIONS: **30 in. x 40 in.**   MEDIUM: **oil on composition board**   DATE: **1931**

ABOUT THE ARTIST: *Grant Wood*

Grant Wood was born on a farm in Iowa in 1891. He was extremely proud of being an American and loved the history and legends of his country. He painted the people of his native Iowa with dignity and gentle humor. He also delighted in painting America's best-loved heroes.

✪ *Questions for Class Discussion*

1 Does this painting depict reality or fantasy? How closely does the painting capture a real colonial town?

Grant Wood is not trying to be historically correct. Instead, he remembers a favorite American poem that his mother recited to him as a young boy. In his painting, Wood tries to re-create the feeling of wonder and enchantment that he first felt upon hearing Henry Wadsworth Longfellow's "Paul Revere's Ride." Here is part of the last stanza:

> So through the night rode Paul Revere;
> And so through the night went his cry of alarm
> To every Middlesex village and farm....
> In the hour of darkness and peril and need,
> The people will waken and listen to hear
> The hurrying hoofbeats of that steed,
> And the midnight message of Paul Revere.

2 Why is Paul Revere riding at midnight? What is his message?

Paul Revere is riding at midnight because he has just heard that the British will be attacking Concord, Massachusetts. The message he shouts, "To arms, to arms!" warns the American minutemen to prepare for battle.

3 What does the tallest building in the painting represent?

The steepled church on the left resembles the Old North Church. It was from this church tower that the signaling lanterns were hung.

4 What might be going on in the well-lit houses?

In the glow of light, the newly awakened citizens are preparing to march off to fight for their liberty from the British.

5 What makes us feel that we are far above the village?

Wood painted this town with dollhouse-sized buildings and tiny people. The chimney tops in the foreground lead our eyes to the repeated patterns of the roofs. We seem to soar up and over the miniature village.

6 What role does the moon play in this painting?

Although we cannot see the moon, its rays light the path Paul Revere must follow, creating dramatic shadows along the way.

7 How many people can you find? How are they dressed?

In response to Revere's warning, ten people appear in windows, in doorways, and in the road. Some are wearing nightclothes.

8 How would you describe Revere's horse?

The artist painted the horse with outstretched legs as though it were flying along the road. It is said that the artist used a wooden rocking horse as a model.

9 How would you describe the shape of the road?

The large circular path that ribbons its way across the painting shows the distance that Revere must travel in order to spread the alarm. It makes us focus on the village within its borders.

10 What are the small lights that snake their way down from the right edge of the painting?

They might represent one of the British patrols eager to catch Paul Revere and stop him.

A Minuteman Speaks

My name is Sylvanus Parker, and I was in my twenty-first year when talk of revolution began. There wasn't a man or woman in our village who wasn't expecting big trouble. Every few days, the sound of the fife and drum would be heard across the village green. It was a signal to stop what you were doing, grab your musket, and join your fellow patriots for training.

Mind you, not one of us is a professional soldier. We are farmers. We work hard, and we love our country. Is it any wonder that we would do anything to win our freedom? Now we are minutemen, ready for action at a minute's notice.

I'll never forget the afternoon my father and I met Paul Revere and the other bigwigs at the Green Dragon Tavern in Boston. It was a secret meeting, and I was so scared and excited that I was trembling. Mr. Revere wanted a report from my father about the size of the minuteman company in our village. My father assured him that we could be counted on.

So when Mr. Revere's warning, "To arms, to arms!" rang out through our town, we and our neighbors came out into the moonlit night in our nightshirts. We spoke in whispers. We embraced one another. We feared for the fate of our farms and families, but we knew we would defend our rights or die in the attempt.

Discussion Question   **The minutemen were the "underdogs" in their battle against the better-equipped, better-trained British army, yet they were victorious. Can you think of other events when an underdog was victorious?**

✦✦✦✦✦✦✦✦✦✦✦✦✦✦✦✦✦✦✦✦✦✦✦✦✦✦✦✦✦✦✦✦✦✦✦✦✦

Business Cards

You might know that Paul Revere built a factory where iron was cast into cannons and bells, ran a mill for rolling copper into sheets that were used to make pots and pans, and was a silversmith and goldsmith. But did you know that he was also a dentist? Seven years before he made his midnight ride, Revere advertised his dental services by printing his business card in the Boston *Gazette* newspaper. The card appears below.

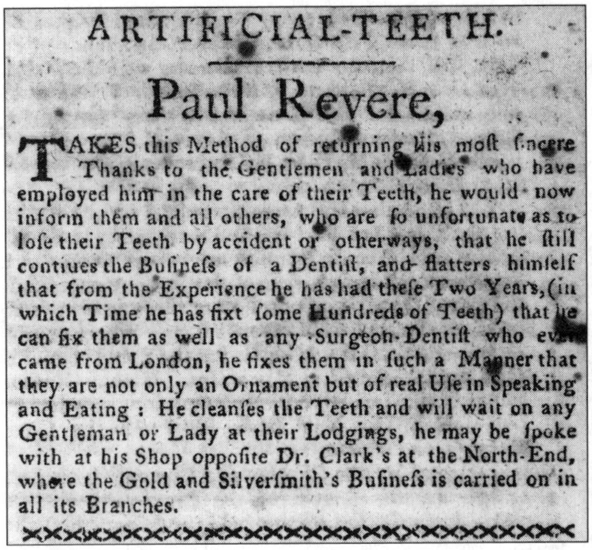

ARTIFICIAL-TEETH.

Paul Revere,

TAKES this Method of returning his moſt ſincere Thanks to the Gentlemen and Ladies who have employed him in the care of their Teeth, he would now inform them and all others, who are ſo unfortunate as to loſe their Teeth by accident or otherways, that he ſtill contiues the Buſineſs of a Dentiſt, and flatters himſelf that from the Experience he has had theſe Two Years, (in which Time he has fixt ſome Hundreds of Teeth) that he can fix them as well as any Surgeon-Dentiſt who ever came from London, he fixes them in ſuch a Manner that they are not only an Ornament but of real Uſe in Speaking and Eating : He cleanſes the Teeth and will wait on any Gentleman or Lady at their Lodgings, he may be ſpoke with at his Shop oppoſite Dr. Clark's at the North-End, where the Gold and Silverſmith's Buſineſs is carried on in all its Branches.

Massachusetts Historical Society

Make your own business card as though you were living in the time of Paul Revere. Choose any profession or occupation of the time—such as candle maker, lamplighter, milkmaid, or seaman. Try using the ornate penmanship, popular in the 1700s, from the sample alphabet below. (Note that in some eighteenth-century words our letter *s* appears as *f*.)

abcdefghijklmnopqrſsstuvwxyz 1234567890 & ? ! $ ¢
ABCDEFGHIJKLMNOPQRSTUVWXYZ

Name_____ Date _____

The British Are Coming!

Track the patriots as they alert the colonists that the British are coming.
Follow these directions and write in your answers at the bottom of the sheet.

1. Paul Revere's starting point, the Old North Church in Boston, is located where line H meets line 12 (the point is called H 12).

   a. Show Revere's trail to G 12. Label that point Charlestown.

   b. Continue Revere's trail to E 10. Label that point Medford.

   c. Continue Revere's trail to C 6. Mark that point Lexington.

   d. Continue Revere's trail to C 4, where Revere is captured. Mark this point with an X.

2. Follow William Dawes's route from Boston to Lexington and up to the point where he was captured by the British.

3. Follow the route of another patriot, Dr. Samuel Prescott, who began his ride at Lexington and made it to Concord.

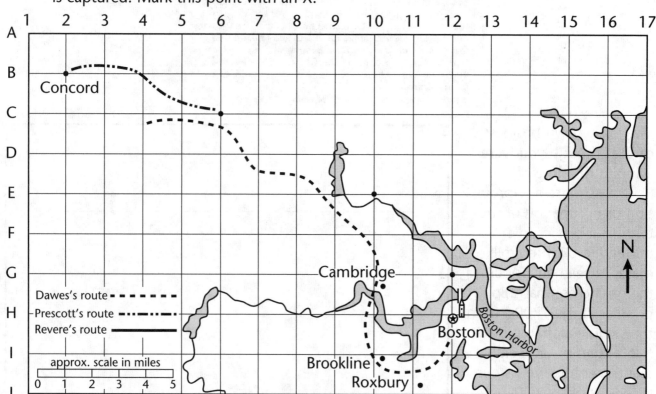

Use a piece of string to measure the patriots' routes.

4. How long was Revere's route? _____

5. About how long was Dawes's route? _____

6. How long was Prescott's route? _____

⭐ Cartoons

Show students Ben Franklin's famous "Join, or Die" snake cartoon. Ask them to name the parts of America represented by the segments of the snake. Suggest that they use research tools, if necessary, to determine which colonies were included in NE (New England). Then invite students to create their own cartoons to illustrate one of the following beliefs:

a. The colonists must unite.

b. The colonists are angry at the British.

⭐ Well-Rounded Men

Paul Revere, Thomas Jefferson, and Benjamin Franklin were men of many talents. Although they were all active in working for America's independence, they had many other interests and hobbies. Ask students to research their other contributions to American life and fill in the chart.

Patriot	Inventions	Hobbies	Other Contributions
Benjamin Franklin			
Thomas Jefferson			
Paul Revere			

⭐ Poetry

Henry Wadsworth Longfellow's poem "Paul Revere's Ride" made Revere famous to generations of Americans. Ask students to write a poem about one or more adventures of a person they admire.

⭐ Quotations

Students can use various reference materials to match these speakers with their quotations.

1. About to be hanged as a spy, this person said, "I only regret that I have but one life to give for my country."

2. In a letter, this person wrote, "Remember the ladies."

3. This statesperson warned, "We must indeed all hang together, or most assuredly we shall all hang separately."

4. In a persuasive pamphlet, this person wrote, "These are the times that try men's souls."

___ Abigail Adams

___ Benjamin Franklin

___ Thomas Paine

___ Nathan Hale

FIGHT BACK, GEORGE!

NEWTOWN, PENNSYLVANIA, DECEMBER 10, 1776 — General Washington and his army have been in retreat for the past four months. The British are sure that the patriots have little fight left in them. *Now is the time to fight back, George! The British are in hot pursuit.*

WHAT IS WASHINGTON'S PLAN?

DECEMBER 20, 1776 — Sixteen large Durham freight boats and four flat ferryboats were moved to General Washington's new headquarters on the Pennsylvania side of the Delaware River. Encamped on the other side, in Trenton, are the Hessians, the German soldiers hired by the British to fight the colonists. It appears certain that Washington will attack. But when?

NO PROOF ABOUT THE TOOTH

It is common knowledge that George Washington's teeth began to fall out when he was a very young man. Dentists have been trying to replace his natural teeth with everything from gold and hippopotamus ivory to elks' and pigs' teeth, but nothing gives him any comfort. Some sets of teeth have been made with springs that force his mouth open. Now, the rumor is that wooden pegs have been placed in his gums to serve as teeth, but that statement cannot be proved.

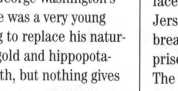

VICTORY OR DEATH

CHRISTMAS NIGHT, 1776 — There was much excitement in the air tonight. Washington's forces of twenty-four hundred men, two hundred horses, and eighteen cannons moved into position on the riverbank. Under the cover of darkness, the troops silently crossed the Delaware River to surprise the Hessians in the Battle of Trenton. Washington has given the password: "Victory or Death."

The following diary entries by an officer on Washington's staff have been made available to us:

December 25, Six p.m.
The wind beats in the faces of the men. It will be a terrible night for the soldiers who have no shoes. Some of them have tied old rags around their feet; others are barefoot, but I have not heard a man complain.

December 26, three a.m.
The men have had a hard time forcing the boats through the floating ice. I never have seen Washington so determined as he is now. He stands on the bank of the river, wrapped in his cloak, superintending the landing of his troops. The storm is changing to sleet and cuts like a knife. The last cannon is being landed, and we are ready to mount our horses.

WON IN ONE HOUR

December 26, 1776 — The freezing, tired men now faced a painful nine-mile march to Trenton, New Jersey, where the Hessians are encamped. At daybreak, they reach the outskirts of Trenton. The surprised Hessians are no match for the Americans. The battle lasts only one hour. There are no American casualties. The Hessian commander, Colonel Johann Rall, dies from his wounds. The first real victory of the war brings strength and optimism to the patriotic cause.

Nine hundred and eighteen Hessians are captured as prisoners of war. Washington's orders to treat the captives fairly result in many Hessians deciding to remain in America and become loyal citizens.

THE LENNOXTOWN INN

The weary traveler is made welcome at our cheerful and comfortable inn. The fireplace is always lit for your convenience.

4 pence a night for a bed.
If supper is requested, 6 pence.
No more than 5 may sleep in one bed.
No dogs allowed upstairs.
No boots to be worn in bed!

ADS & COMMERCIAL NOTICES

VIRGINIA COBBLER Tradesperson who has designed shoes for the dainty feet of Mrs. Martha Washington announces the opening of his new shoe store. A large supply of hand-carved high heels in the French style are available. Located on Water Street in the business section of Richmond, not far from the State House.

WEATHER REPORT: December 25, 1776— Snow, sleet, freezing rain; cold, biting winds; temperatures well below freezing

PITY THE POOR REDCOAT

The uniform that the British soldier is forced to wear is guaranteed to produce a rash, a sore neck, sunstroke, and leg cramps. British officers believe that the more uncomfortable a soldier is, the angrier he will get, and the harder he will fight.

The woolen coat with its metal buttons, heavy lining, and yards of lace is itchy and weighs too much.

The leather collar rubs against the poor soldier's neck until it bleeds, and the knee breeches are so tight that they cause numbness in the legs. How different from the uniforms of our American soldiers!

OOPS!   July 4, 1776 — British King George III writes in his diary: "Not much happened today."

The Lighter Side of the News

- George Washington is fond of ice cream. The kitchen at his home in Mount Vernon contains pewter and tin ice cream pots.
- After a battle in Pennsylvania, a dog was discovered in the American camp. It was wearing a collar showing that its owner was the British Commander, General Howe. The next day, an American soldier, holding a white flag in one hand and the dog in the other, crossed over to the British side and returned the dog. General Washington expressed his pleasure that the animal was returned to its owner.

1776 YEAR-END REPORT

Here are some highlights:

MARCH 23: **Patrick Henry** delivers a moving speech to the Virginia legislature concluding with the rousing "Give me liberty, or give me death!"

JUNE 15: **George Washington** becomes commander in chief of the Continental Army. He chooses to receive no pay but advises that he will later submit an expense account.

JULY 26: The Second Continental Congress votes for a postal system. **Benjamin Franklin** is chosen as postmaster general.

AUGUST: The first submarine, called the ***Turtle***, attempts to place explosives on a British ship docked in New York Harbor. The mission fails, but the *Turtle* and its one-man crew escape.

THE PICTURE TELLS A STORY
Washington Crossing the Delaware

DIMENSIONS: 149 in. x 255 in.   **MEDIUM:** oil on canvas   **DATE:** 1851

ABOUT THE ARTIST: *Emanuel Gottlieb Leutze*

Seventy-five years after the event, the German-born artist Emanuel Gottlieb Leutze (LOYT-se) made this enormous painting. Leutze never meant to create a historical document. Instead, he sought to capture both the spirit and drama of an important time in America's history.

When Leutze had visited America at the age of nine, stories of George Washington captured his imagination. Leutze never saw Washington, but he had a lifelong admiration for the man as a symbol of liberty and freedom. Although this painting was done in Germany, it is interesting to note that Leutze used Americans as models for all but one of the soldiers in the boat. The popular appeal of *Washington Crossing the Delaware* has made it one of the most famous paintings in America.

⭐ *Questions for Class Discussion*

1 Which person in the boat do you notice first?

George Washington is undoubtedly the most important person in this massive painting. At a height of six feet two inches, he alone stands tall and confident. The gold color of the sky behind him lights up his face as he calmly stares at his destination—the enemy across the river.

2 How does George Washington's pose add to his importance?

He stands as still as a statue with one foot forward. His high-booted feet are planted firmly in the boat. He does not struggle to keep his balance.

3 How does George Washington's uniform differ from those of the other soldiers?

Washington looks important because he is dressed in a very grand style, suitable for the commander in chief. In contrast, the other men are wearing an assortment of their own jackets and hats. It was not until two years after this incident that regulation uniforms were provided for the Continental soldiers.

4 What are the two objects that Washington is carrying?

An ornate sword hangs at his side, while his right hand holds a small telescope, called a spyglass.

5 What elements in the painting suggest severe weather?

The dark water, clogged with moving blocks of ice, seems nearly impassable. The wintry light creates a mood of extreme danger. In the boat, the flag flies wildly in the wind, and a soldier struggles to keep his hat from blowing away. Can you find the sick soldier who huddles to keep from freezing?

6 Who are the other people in the boat?

They represent a cross section of the American population—farmers, wealthy gentlemen, young boys, and older men. The oarsmen are soldiers from Marblehead, Massachusetts, who were actually experienced sailors and fishermen. The black man in the boat is Prince Whipple. During the Revolutionary War, he was a bodyguard to George Washington. The young soldier holding the flag is Colonel James Monroe. He later became the fifth President of the United States.

7 What activities are taking place in the boat?

Washington is the calm within the storm. Everything else appears to be in motion. A man in front uses a pole to fight off the floating ice. Several men clutch the icy oars in an attempt to row, while two others struggle to keep the flag aloft. The man in the rear uses a rudder to steer. Each soldier turns in a different direction, focusing only on doing the job at hand. This journey across the Delaware River is a tense battle between humans and the forces of nature.

8 What is happening in the other boats?

A long line of boats and men can be seen in the distance. You can almost hear the high-pitched neighing of the frightened horses. The men, too, are all in motion. Some try to calm the horses; others frantically guide the boats against the currents of the hostile river.

9 Where is the morning star?

It appears in the sky above the front of Washington's boat. The boat heads in the direction of the emerging light. As the boat moves forward, the darkness is left behind. The dawn of a new day is coming.

10 How accurate is the painting?

There are many historical errors, but they do not detract from the success of the painting. For one thing, the boats shown in this painting were not the types of boats used by Washington. Washington actually used long, high-sided Durham boats. Each held about forty men. Raftlike flat boats were reserved for horses and cannons.

Another historical error involves the American flag. The flag with stars and stripes was first adopted by Congress on June 14, 1777, and would not have been used at the Battle of Trenton. Furthermore, instead of flying the flag on a stormy night, the men would have rolled and encased it to keep it safe.

In addition, the Marblehead oarsmen would have been wearing their blue jackets, white caps, and tarred (waterproofed) pants. And common sense tells us that George Washington would not have been standing in such a small boat.

A Marblehead Fisherman Speaks

Aye, it is no secret that we Marblehead men are rough. Life at sea has taught us to face danger without flinching, and I must say that we are real proud of our reputations. Have you ever visited Marblehead? It lies four miles south of Salem, Massachusetts. If you're not interested in fishing, you needn't bother coming. Life may not be easy here, but it is the life we have freely chosen. We have made our mark in this new land by drying and curing fish, which we sell at a good profit to the rest of New England and even to Europe. There is no better fisherman alive than a Marblehead fisherman.

Now, you've probably guessed that old King George wasn't about to sit around and watch us prosper. He began to pile one tax upon another. One law allowed the British to board and search any vessel they pleased without requesting permission to do so. In 1775, the British passed a new law that prevented us New Englanders from using our best fishing grounds. "By King George!" we roared. "You've gone too far!" We began to form our own militia (army of citizens), and we trained four times a week. We were ready, willing, and able to defend our liberties. After all, we were men who could handle muskets as well as oars. And what a sight we made as we marched off to war in our blue jackets with leather buttons, our white caps, and our tarred trousers.

Discussion Question

The men from Marblehead made their living as fishermen. But when they were needed, they volunteered to secure boats and navigate the dangerous waters. Their skills helped win the Battle of Trenton. Think of another group—perhaps a contemporary group—that has offered to help others and made a difference because of that help.

Name _____ Date _____

GEORGE III

George vs. George

King George III of England and General George Washington of America led their countries during the Revolutionary War. The chart below gives information about the British George. Use books and electronic sources to research facts about the American George. Fill in as much information as you can.

GEORGE WASHINGTON

DATE OF BIRTH June 4, 1738

PARENTS Frederick Lewis (prince of Wales) and Augusta, daughter of Frederick (duke of Saxe-Gotha)

FAMILY HOME Windsor Castle

WIFE Princess Charlotte of Mecklenburg

DATE OF MARRIAGE September 8, 1761

CHILDREN 15

OCCUPATION king

HAIR COLOR auburn

HEIGHT tall

WEIGHT about 14 stone (196 pounds)

HOBBIES backgammon; collecting locks, coins, and model ships; astronomy; music

FAVORITE FOODS fresh fruit and sauerkraut; mutton with turnips

ILLNESSES porphyria, a disease that affected his mind

DRESS did not care about fashion

GREATEST PROBLEM the American colonies

DIED January 27, 1820, at age eighty-one

DATE OF BIRTH _____

PARENTS _____

_____

FAMILY HOME _____

WIFE _____

DATE OF MARRIAGE _____

CHILDREN _____

OCCUPATION _____

HAIR COLOR _____

HEIGHT _____

WEIGHT _____

HOBBIES _____

_____

FAVORITE FOODS _____

_____

ILLNESSES _____

DRESS _____

GREATEST PROBLEM _____

DIED _____

Dialogue

Washington Crossing the Delaware

Here is a sketch of George Washington and some of the men from the painting. Together they crossed the Delaware on the stormy night of Christmas 1776. The blurb for each soldier gives you insights into his character. For each man, write in the bubble the words he might have spoken during the crossing.

1 Prince Whipple
Black oarsman at the left side of boat. Whipple was born in Africa. As a child he was sent by his parents to America to be educated but wound up being sold into slavery. His owner, General Whipple, arranged for him to become Washington's bodyguard. After the war, Prince Whipple won his freedom.

2 George Washington
Commander in chief of the Continental Army. On this night Washington desperately needed to inspire his weary army to fight for the cause of freedom.

3 James Monroe
Young colonel who holds the flag. Once in Trenton, Monroe led the charge and captured two enemy guns. He was hit in the shoulder by a cannonball. Later, Monroe became the fifth President of the United States.

4 Seafaring Man of Marblehead
One of the Massachusetts men angered by British laws that interfered with the colonists' right to fish. The men formed a regiment under General John Glover. On this night of battle, the men of Marblehead helped get soldiers and equipment across the river.

5 Sick Soldier
Despite hunger, freezing weather, and illness, the soldiers remained loyal to Washington and put aside their personal needs to fight for freedom.

✪ Flag Waving

At one time, each of the thirteen colonies had its own flag. On January 2, 1776, the first flag of the United States was raised in Massachusetts by George Washington. This flag did not have the stars and stripes that we know today. Ask students to describe what this flag looked like as they research the growth of the American flag from its beginnings in Massachusetts to its present form. Then give students the opportunity to design their own flags or banners to represent their class, school, club, or team.

✪ A Royal USA?

George Washington was offered the title King of the United States, but he turned it down. If George Washington had accepted the title, how different might America be today?

✪ Washington's Orders

George Washington had ordered supplies for the Battle of Trenton but realized that the weather was going to prevent their arrival. Nevertheless, he wanted to make certain that his army behaved as gentlemen and did not take what didn't belong to them. Read aloud Washington's orders to his troops:

> His Excellency General George Washington strictly forbids all the officers and soldiers of the Continental Army . . . [from] plundering any person whatsoever. It is expected that humanity and tenderness to women and children will distinguish brave Americans . . . from the British or Hessians.

Ask students to find in their local newspaper examples of an organized group that has shown concern or kindness for others.

✪ Revolutionary Women

Guide students to sources that will help them research and present an oral report on one of the following women: Abigail Adams, Molly Pitcher, Deborah Samson.

✪ I Spy

John Honeyman, Benedict Arnold, and John André were famous spies of the Revolutionary War. Ask students to research the secrets they discovered and how they changed the course of the war.

SEQUOYA AND THE "TALKING LEAVES"

NEW ECHOTA, GEORGIA, 1828 — The *Cherokee Phoenix*, the first newspaper of the Cherokee people, has been published to great acclaim. It is reported that businesspeople and politicians in Washington, D.C., as well as Cherokee are reading the paper every week. This four-page paper is printed in two languages: English and Cherokee. The Cherokee alphabet was invented only seven years ago by a Cherokee scholar named Sequoya.

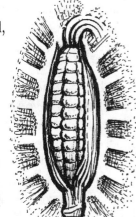

Sequoya had noticed that white men had the magic of capturing speech on paper with tiny black ink marks. Sequoya called these papers "talking leaves." He decided to make Cherokee talking leaves so that his people could communicate with one another in a written language. *Within a few years of Sequoya's invention, half the Cherokee could read and write.*

THE GREEN CORN CEREMONY

FALL 1829 — The Green Corn ceremony was once again a highlight in the Cherokee year—a time to show respect for the corn that is so vital to Cherokee life.

Entire villages were cleaned, and all broken pottery was mended. Neighbors made an effort to settle disputes. The Cherokee always symbolize a new start by putting out all the old fires in each village and then relighting them with a newly lit flame. At the ceremony, Cherokee elders danced around the new flame, which must be kept alive throughout the winter.

GOLD DISCOVERED ON CHEROKEE LAND

GEORGIA, 1829 — The cry of "Gold!" rang through the hills of Georgia this year. Overcome with gold fever, tens of thousands of white men stampeded into Cherokee Nation lands, and the Georgia militia ordered the Cherokee from their homes. *Those who refused to leave were beaten or killed.* The Cherokee protested this unfair treatment to the Supreme Court. Chief Justice John Marshall sided with them. The overjoyed Cherokee celebrated their victory, but it did not last. President Andrew Jackson, longtime enemy of the Indians, said that he would never enforce the Supreme Court ruling.

Ward; Baldwin/Corbis-Bettmann

This poster accuses President Jackson of commanding too much power. Here his foot is actually trampling the United States Constitution.

Did You Know That...?

- The giant redwood trees in California are named after Sequoya, the man who invented a written language for the Cherokee people.

THE TRAIL OF TEARS

GEORGIA, 1838 — Army General Winfield Scott and his seven thousand men brutally searched out every home and seized Cherokee as prisoners. Men, women, and children were rounded up like cattle and marched off to stockades. For many months, the Cherokee remained imprisoned in filth and heat. Hundreds died from sickness and starvation.

Then seventeen thousand Cherokee, many sick and elderly, began a forced journey west. They were going to their new homeland in Oklahoma, which was eight hundred miles away. More than four thousand Cherokee dropped from hunger, cold, and exhaustion alongside the road. Silently, they were buried in shallow graves along what came to be known as the Trail of Tears. A United States soldier who had seen much violence in his life said, "The Cherokee removal was the cruelest work I ever saw."

Fabulous Firsts 1838–1848

- **John Deere** manufactures the first plow designed for prairie soil.

- **Mt. Holyoke Seminary,** the first college exclusively for women, opens in Massachusetts with an enrollment of 116 women.
- **Oberlin College** in Ohio admits four women on an equal basis with men. Oberlin is also the first college in the U.S. to admit qualified blacks.
- **Samuel F. B. Morse** files a patent on his new invention, the telegraph.
- Building of the **Washington Monument** has begun. It is designed in the shape of a hollow obelisk of ancient Egypt. When it is completed, the monument will be over 555 feet high.

SOME EASTERN CHEROKEE REMAIN

According to Cherokee accounts, a native named Tsali killed a U.S. soldier who had attacked Tsali's wife. After Tsali escaped to the mountains, the Army sent word to him. If he would give himself up, the other Cherokee hiding in the hills would be left alone.

To save his people, Tsali surrendered and was sentenced to death. As promised, his people were unharmed, and Tsali's descendants continue to live in the North Carolina Smoky Mountains. They represent the eastern branch of the Cherokee Nation.

PERSONALS

Join Roper's Gym Have you exchanged your healthy life on the farm for the shut-up life of a city office? Are you nervous because you do not get any exercise? Are you stiff jointed, soft muscled, and pale complexioned? Then, join Roper's Gym in Philadelphia, a first-class establishment to assist you in regaining your health. Don't wait! Our facility is located in the heart of the city at 704 State Street, third floor, rear.

Looking for a Bride Ambitious young man, thirty years of age, looking for a strong woman willing to live in Ohio. She should be able to spin thread, weave cloth, sew clothes, keep a garden, and cook. Also must be able to make cheese, candles, soap, and butter. Idle hands need not apply. Address your reply to The Daily News, Box 11, 4 Fletcher Drive, Cleveland, Ohio.

The Latest Dance Craze Are you a wallflower? Do you sit alone while your friends enjoy the thrilling dance import from Europe? **Learn to waltz.** Mr. Horace Golightly will teach you all the new steps for a modest fee. Address your inquiries to the Starlight Dance Studio, 3 Wren Street, Newark, New Jersey.

THE PICTURE TELLS A STORY
The Trail of Tears

dimensions: 64 in. x 42 in.   medium: Oil on canvas   date: 1942

ABOUT THE ARTIST: *Robert Lindneux*

The artist Robert Lindneux was born in New York City in 1871 and studied art in Europe. When he came back to America, he fell in love with Western subjects. Before he would start a painting, he would research an event, speak to old-timers, and place the scene in its correct historical setting.

⭐ *Questions for Class Discussion*

1 How does the artist show the Cherokees' sadness?

The people's faces are filled with pain. Many of them have bowed their heads in despair. Even the animals seem to be miserable.

2 What information does the painting provide about the weather?

Low, dark clouds indicate the beginnings of a storm, and the rising wind stirs up puffs of dust. Autumn colors dot the prairie region that the Cherokee are passing through, but the people hold their blankets tightly around their bodies to keep warm. A trace of light shines in the sky behind them, but they are forced to struggle westward into the darkness. In fact, the first group of Cherokee set out on their eight-hundred-mile trip on October 1, 1838, and unusually harsh fall weather added to the hardships of their journey.

3 What kind of transportation did the Cherokee use for the trip?

Horses, mules, and oxen pulled the Cherokees' six hundred wagons. Yet there was not enough room in the wagons for everyone. Hundreds, including women and children, were forced to make the journey on foot. Some of the women carried their children or large bundles on their backs for the entire journey.

4 The Cherokee had to make quick decisions about what to carry with them. What do you think they took?

When they were rounded up, the Cherokee packed corn, beans, and squash, as well as dried meat. But this food was used up even before their traveling began, and the salt pork, corn, and coffee provided by the government was often unfit to eat. Starvation was common. The government was supposed to provide an iron cooking pot and blankets for each family. In the confusion, many received nothing. In haste, some Indians grabbed bedding and cooking utensils, but most possessions were left behind.

5 What sounds would you hear if you were on this difficult march?

The Cherokee call this journey "Nunna-dual-tsunyi," meaning "the trail where we cried." The sounds of moaning children, the sick, and the old never seemed to stop. They mingled with the creaking of the wagon wheels, the barking of the dogs, and the howling of the wind across the land.

6 Who in the painting carried weapons?

The Cherokee were escorted by both the native police and American troops. Notice the three armed guards in the left foreground of the painting.

Clarissa Speaks

When the soldiers broke into our house and told us to leave, I began to cry. Mother grabbed my hand and said, "Clarissa, we will cry later. Now we must decide what to take with us." My little brother didn't hesitate. He clutched his brown-and-white dog. Mother was rushing around, picking up food, bedding, a cooking pot, some clothing. I had never seen her so confused. She strapped the wooden cradleboard to her back to hold my baby sister, who was only five months old.

The soldiers began to push us out. I couldn't make a decision. Every object in the house seemed to say, "Take me, take me." I grabbed a red shawl and a blank writing tablet to use as a diary. I will write in it every day. Everyone who reads it will never forget the story of my people.

My grandfather used to say, "Our land was so beautiful, the white man wants to take it for his own." He thought that if we became more like the white people, they would respect us. Everyone in our family dressed in American-style clothing. We lived in a white house with a fence around it. I don't like to brag, but I can read and write in both Cherokee and English.

But nothing we did impressed the settlers. When the day of removal finally came, the soldiers forced us away with the tips of their bayonets. I turned back for one last look at our home. I saw a white family carrying out my furniture and clothing. Then I saw them set our house on fire. For the first time, I realized I could *never, never* go back.

Discussion Question

If you were suddenly forced to leave your home, what would you take with you? What would be your fears and concerns?

Map Study

1. Many states still have their original Indian names. On the map showing the states through which the Cherokee passed on their journey from Georgia to the Oklahoma Territory, write in the missing state names. Here are clues:

a. The name of this state means "great river." Montgomery's Point was along the water route through which some of the Cherokee traveled.

b. According to Indians, this state's name means "bend in the river." Nashville is the state capital.

c. The name of this state means "muddy water." Springfield and Jackson are two towns in this state.

d. To the Indians, the name of this state means "land of tomorrow." Hopkinsville in this state was on the Trail of Tears.

e. The name of this state means "river of men." The town of Golconda in this state was on the Trail of Tears.

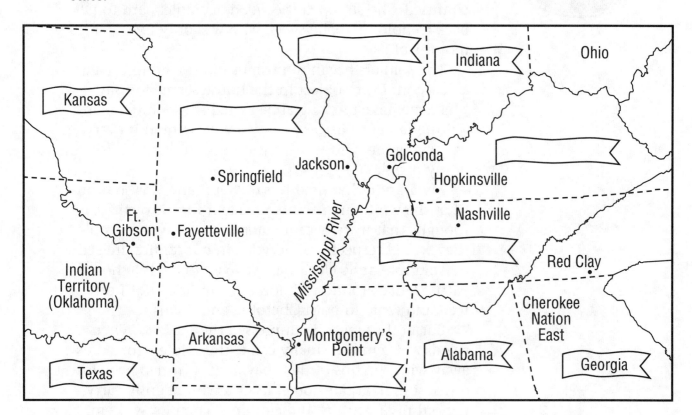

2. The Cherokee took many land and water routes to Oklahoma. On the map, mark one of the land routes by following these directions:

a. Begin in Red Clay.

b. Continue to Nashville.

c. Cross the border to Hopkinsville.

d. Go through Golconda.

e. Continue on to Jackson and Springfield.

f. Move down to Fayetteville.

g. Cross the border to Fort Gibson in Indian Territory.

Original Poetry

The Cherokee had great respect for nature. They honored the seasons, mountains, valleys, rivers, plants, and animals. One way to honor nature is to write about it. Below is a diamonte, a special form of poetry. The directions for writing appear on the left, and a sample, called "Winter," appears on the right. After you've studied the directions and the sample, try writing two diamontes of your own in the spaces provided.

Line 1: Write a noun related to nature. . . . . Winter

Line 2: Write two adjectives. . . . . Blustery, frozen

Line 3: Write three words ending in *ing*. . . . . Slipping, piercing, shivering

Line 4: Write four nouns. . . . . Blizzard, ice, snowflake, marshmallow

Line 5: Write another three words ending in *ing*. . . . . Skating, sledding, skiing

Line 6: Write another two adjectives. . . . . White, silent

Line 7: Repeat the noun you started with. . . . . Winter

1. _____
2. _____
3. _____
4. _____
5. _____
6. _____
7. _____

1. _____
2. _____
3. _____
4. _____
5. _____
6. _____
7. _____

✪ *History Repeating Itself*

Share with students that the Cherokee were one of several groups of people who were suddenly forced to leave their homeland. For example, the Nez Percé Indians suffered a fate similar to the Cherokee. During the Holocaust in Europe (1939–1944), the Nazis persecuted and murdered six million Jews. More recently, in Bosnia and in parts of Africa, minorities have been forced to flee. Students may select one of these groups and read a related article from a book, newspaper, or magazine. Then they can share with one another what they learned.

✪ *Telling Jokes*

Tell students what Will Rogers, a popular movie star and journalist in the early 1900s, once said about his Cherokee heritage: "My forefathers didn't come over on the *Mayflower*, but they met the boat." Then ask students to look into Will Rogers's life and his rise to fame. Students' goal should be to share some of Rogers's jokes with their classmates.

✪ *More Indian Names*

More than half of the states in the U.S.A. have Indian names. Ask students to match the following states with their original Indian names and meanings.

a. Michigan	___ Yuttahih: "one that is higher up"
b. Kansas	___ Edah hoe: "light on the mountains"
c. Massachusetts	___ Miskonsin: "grassy place"
d. Idaho	___ Mishigamaw: "big lake"
e. Alaska	___ Kanza: "south wind people"
f. Utah	___ Massadchu-es-et: "great hill, small place"
g. Wisconsin	___ Alakshak: "peninsula"

✪ *Mapping*

On an outline map of their state, invite students to indicate rivers, mountains, lakes, and cities that have Indian names.

✪ *Comparing Games*

Tell students that a popular game among the Cherokee was stickball. Each player carried two sticks, between two and three feet long, with a cup at the end designed to hold a ball. Each end of the field had a goal post. The object of the game was to get the ball through the opposition's goal post. Since there were often a hundred players on each team, this was a very rough game. Ask students to tell what contemporary games are similar to Cherokee stickball and to describe their similarities and differences.

FUGITIVE SLAVE LAW PASSED

SEPTEMBER 1850 — A new law about fugitive, or runaway, slaves has just been passed. Now slaves who make it safely to a free state and are caught *must be returned to their owners.* Furthermore, people in free states are *required* to help catch escaped slaves. Any person who helps a slave escape or doesn't cooperate with the slave catchers can be put in jail. Many abolitionists, people who are against slavery, say they will not obey this law.

135,000 SETS, 270,000 VOLUMES SOLD.

UNCLE TOM'S CABIN

FOR SALE HERE.

AN EDITION FOR THE MILLION, COMPLETE IN 1 Vol., PRICE 37 1-2 CENTS.
"   "   IN GERMAN, IN 1 Vol., PRICE 50 CENTS.
"   "   IN 2 Vols,. CLOTH, 6 PLATES, PRICE $1.50.
SUPERB ILLUSTRATED EDITION, IN 1 Vol., WITH 153 ENGRAVINGS,
PRICES FROM $2.50 TO $5.00,

The Greatest Book of the Age.

Culver Pictures

CABIN INFLAMES READERS

BOSTON, MASSACHUSETTS, AUGUST 23,1852 — *Uncle Tom's Cabin,* a novel by Harriet Beecher Stowe, is reaching the hearts and minds of people everywhere. It is already sold out in bookstores in the North. The book's descriptions of hunted and oppressed slaves and cruel masters have caused thousands of Northerners to oppose the Fugitive Slave Law. The book has enraged people in the South and has added to their bitter feelings toward the abolitionists. *Uncle Tom's Cabin* may be the most powerful novel ever written.

UNDERGROUND RAILROAD: A PATH OF PERIL

1852 — The Underground Railroad is not a train, nor does it travel underground. It does not have a recognized leader but is made up of people, both black and white, who are willing to risk their lives by guiding slaves to freedom in the North. The people who lead the slaves are called conductors. The slaves are sometimes referred to as parcels or passengers. The houses where the runaway slaves can safely hide during their long journey are the stations, and the owners of these houses are referred to as stationmasters. A "ticket," such as the one below, is used to pass slaves from one station on the Underground Railroad to another.

A Ticket on the Underground Railroad

Medina, September 6, 1852
Monroe & Peck
Gents, here are five Slaves from the House of Bondage, which I need not say to you that you will see to them — they can tell their own story.
Yours etc.,
H. G. Blake

THE WOMAN CALLED MOSES

Harriet Tubman, who escaped from slavery in 1850, has become a legend and one of the most successful conductors on the Underground Railroad. Over the years, she has guided 300 slaves to freedom. Even though she could have remained safe in the North, she has been returning to the South to lead other slaves to safety.

Tubman is called Moses because, like the biblical leader, she has led her people out of slavery.

Did You Know That...?

- Baseball in the United States dates back to the 1840s. By 1846, the New York Nine and the Knickerbockers were playing four-inning games.

TUBMAN RESCUES KNOWN FUGITIVE

TROY, NEW YORK, APRIL 27, 1859 — At today's trial of John Nalle, a slave who had escaped to the North, Harriet Tubman and others helped the convicted man break through to freedom once again. While on trial under the Fugitive Slave Law, Nalle did not know that the famous Harriet Tubman was sitting in the courtroom disguised as an old lady. Outside, a crowd of a thousand noisy abolitionists was determined to help Nalle escape.

When the federal marshals led Nalle outside, his hands in chains, Tubman gave a signal to the waiting crowd. As soon as Nalle reached the street, a band of black and white abolitionists surrounded him. Tubman grabbed on to Nalle's body and would not let go. The marshals' clubs struck her repeatedly on the head, but she held fast. She and others pulled Nalle through the crowd to safety and freedom.

REWARD FOR THE CAPTURE OF HARRIET TUBMAN

WANTED

$40,000 REWARD

for the capture of HARRIET TUBMAN
Escaped from slavery in 1850
Conductor on the Underground Railroad

Posters have appeared all over the South informing people of a reward from $12,000 to $40,000 for the capture of Harriet Tubman. At least nineteen times, Tubman has returned South to rescue slaves. She has never lost a man, woman, or child.

Song Heard in the Cotton Fields

Rabbit in the briar patch
Squirrel in the tree,
Wish I could go hunting,
But I ain't free.

Did You Know That Harriet Tubman . . . ?

- served as a spy for the Union Army.
- located ammunition hidden by the Confederates.
- served as a nurse to wounded black and white soldiers.
- made her own medicines from roots and herbs.

A TOLL GATE ON THE BALTIMORE-REISTERTOWN ROAD

MARCH 1838 — As traffic has increased in Maryland, people have been demanding new and better roads, and private corporations have begun to respond. The owner of the new road between Baltimore and Reistertown has placed sharp sticks, called pikes, on the gates blocking the entrances to the road. To get on the road, a traveler has to pay a toll, or fee, to the gatekeeper, who then turns the pikes to allow the traveler through. *The turnpike has been born!*

⚫ C L A S S I F I E D   A D S

Help Wanted

Brawny males needed for work at the National Nail factory. National Nail provides handmade nails to attach shoes to horses' hooves. Applicants must withstand extreme heat. Send references to National Nail Co., 36 Broad Street, Cincinnati, Ohio. Attention: Mr. I. M. Hammer.

THE PICTURE TELLS A STORY
Forward

DIMENSIONS: **23⅞ in. x 35¹⁵⁄₁₆ in.**   MEDIUM: **tempera on masonite**   DATE: **1967**

ABOUT THE ARTIST: *Jacob Lawrence*

The black artist Jacob Lawrence was born in New Jersey in 1917. He moved to New York, where he closely observed and dramatically painted the black experience in Harlem. He went on to portray the history of black Americans as they left the South and migrated to the Northern cities. His paintings won wide acclaim for their bold colors and large, flat forms that gave strong expression to the struggle for freedom and justice.

In 1939, he began the Harriet Tubman series that consists of thirty-one panels. Lawrence said, "Exploring the American experience is a beautiful thing. . . . We hear about Molly Pitcher . . . about Betsy Ross. . . . The Negro woman has never been included in American history."[1] In 1967, he wrote and illustrated the children's book *Harriet and the Promised Land*.

⊛ *Questions for Class Discussion*

1 **Who are the people in the painting, and what are they doing?**
They are runaway slaves traveling on the Underground Railroad.

2 **How would you describe them? Do they seem afraid?**
It was not unusual for slaveholders to hire slave catchers to track fugitive slaves with dogs and to offer large rewards for the return of slaves. The pun-

ishment for escaping was often a brutal whipping. Some returned slaves were purposely crippled so that they could never run away again.

In this painting, the man at the end of the line looks behind him in fear. The man at the head of the line has to be urged forward into the unknown. Most slaves had never before left the plantation and must have felt great trepidation while walking at night through dangerous territory.

3 Who is the woman pushing the first man forward?

She is Harriet Tubman, a former slave and the most famous conductor on the Underground Railroad.

4 What is she holding in her hand?

Harriet Tubman always carried a pistol for self-defense. She once said, "There was one of two things I had a right to, liberty or death. If I could not have one, I would have the other, for no man should take me alive. I should fight for my liberty as long as my strength lasted!" She also carried the gun to discourage any timid runaways from giving up and going back. She feared that a frightened returning slave might reveal the secrets of the Underground Railroad to the slaveholder and place many people's lives in jeopardy.

5 How does the brown landscape on which the runaways travel add to the feeling of danger?

The mass of dark brown dips to the right. We cannot tell if it represents a mountain pass, a field, or farmland. Because the place is so hard to identify, it adds to the painting's tone of danger.

6 How can you determine whether it is night or day in the painting?

The deep blue sky in the background seems to indicate that it is night. Logically, the safest time for fugitives to travel through unfriendly territory was nighttime.

7 What do you think the circle in the top right corner is?

The circle is probably the North Star. The black abolitionist Frederick Douglass, a friend of Tubman's, paid tribute to the years she spent leading her people through the woods and swamps with only the North Star and her own good sense to guide her. He said, "The midnight sky and silent stars have been the witnesses of your devotion to freedom and of your heroism."

8 What is the woman behind Harriet Tubman carrying in her arms?

She clutches a baby. Very few female slaves would try to escape without their children, but children made the passage to freedom much more difficult. If they cried or if they could not keep up with the other fugitives, they could endanger everybody. Tubman carried a sleeping medicine that she would use to quiet a crying child.

9 Why are the people in the painting barefoot?

It is a fact that many slaves did not own shoes. A Quaker named Thomas Garrett, who became one of Tubman's closest friends, owned a shoe store in Wilmington, Delaware. Not only was his house a station on the Underground Railroad, but he also gave a pair of shoes to each runaway he sheltered. Quite probably, Harriet Tubman, who had lived in the North, owned her own shoes, but Jacob Lawrence chose to paint her barefoot.

10 What did the escaping slaves eat on this journey from the South to the North?

They were probably hungry most of the time. They sometimes might find apples, berries, and corn; they might catch a fish in a river. Some stationmasters provided a meal for slaves who stayed with them. But most of the runaways were used to hardships and accepted them as the price of freedom.

---

¹ Ellen Harkins Wheat, *Jacob Lawrence, American Painter* (University of Washington Press, 1994)

Dulcie Speaks

I feel like a stranger everywhere. There is no place that feels like home. But where I'm now is better than where I'm coming from. I'm in a house in a country called Canada, and a kind lady is writing down the words for me. I wish I knew the secret of reading and writing, but education never reached me.

All my life—until now—I've been somebody's property. I've been beaten and insulted and there was never a day when I didn't tremble like a leaf in the wind.

I once had a strong husband, Enoch, and he was a good man. Last year, he was sold farther south to the cotton fields. Our master was having money troubles, and he began to sell off some of his slaves. I knew that once I had my baby, we would be the next to be sold. Then I heard that Moses was in Maryland. I sent word that I needed help, and I prayed she would listen. I feared she wouldn't consider me because I had such a young baby to carry along. But Moses can do anything! She led us to the places that were safe and kept us away from those that weren't. I can't describe how frightened we were and how we suffered from the long, long journey.

I pray that soon someone who reads what is written here will know my husband, Enoch, and will tell him that his wife, Dulcie, and his baby are alive and well and miss him.

Discussion Question   **Now that Dulcie is free, what problems does she face?**

Name _____ Date _____

Stitching a Path to Freedom

Sewing together scraps of cloth into a design or a picture is called patchwork. Patchwork quilts were often used by members of the Underground Railroad to identify a safe station. If the color black was hung on a clothesline, escaping slaves would know they had reached a safe house.

This patchwork says, "Keep to the path alongside the railroad tracks."

The black sheep in this patchwork identifies a safe station.

The Big Dipper points to the North Star and the way to freedom.

In the squares below, draw pictures to illustrate these messages:

This house is no longer a safe station.

You must follow the river to the waiting wagon.

Stamp of Approval

Harriet Tubman, Harriet Beecher Stowe, and Frederick Douglass all worked to end slavery. More recently, people such as Rosa Parks and Martin Luther King Jr. have fought for the dignity of black Americans.

1. Select a civil rights leader you admire. On the lines below, draft a short letter to the postmaster general of the United States. State reasons that this person should be honored on a stamp.

Dear Postmaster General:

_____

_____

_____

_____

_____

_____

_____

2. In the rectangle on the right, design and color a stamp for the person you selected.

✪ *Research and Informal Debate*

Introduce the figure of John Brown, an abolitionist who, in 1858, raided a U.S. arsenal in Harpers Ferry, in what is now West Virginia. His goal was to arm slaves. Brown was captured, found guilty, and sentenced to death. Tell students that some people thought that John Brown was a dangerous man while others believed he was a hero. Encourage students to find and read sources about the raid on Harpers Ferry. Then in a class discussion elicit from students reasons for pro-Brown and anti-Brown positions.

✪ *Research and Panel Discussion*

In Ferrisburgh, Vermont, there is an historic house called Rokeby. More than one hundred years ago, it was a station on the Underground Railroad. The original owner, Rowland Thomas Robinson, was a Quaker abolitionist. He and his family gave room and board to slaves who needed their help. In some cases, fugitives who spent long periods of time with the Robinsons were taught to read and write.

Ask students to find more information about the Underground Railroad. Ask the groups specifically to find out about stationmasters other than Robinson and conductors other than Tubman. After the groups complete their work, have them participate in a panel discussion on these heroes of the antislavery movement.

✪ *Codes*

Students will enjoy learning that the spiritual "Follow the Drinking Gourd" contains a code, or hidden instructions, to guide runaway slaves to safety. According to researchers, the gourd in the song refers to the Big Dipper, which points to the North Star, which in turn points in the direction of freedom for the slaves. Some people think "old man" in the song stands for Peg Leg Joe, a conductor on the Underground Railroad; others think "old man" refers to the Mississippi River. Here is a one stanza of the song.

> When the great big river meets the little river,
> Follow the drinking gourd.
> For the old man is a-waiting for to carry you to freedom
> If you follow the drinking gourd.

Invite students to write a poem or a song that contains a secret message about something that is important to them.

ABRAHAM LINCOLN ELECTED PRESIDENT

NOVEMBER 15, 1860 — Abraham Lincoln has been elected the sixteenth President of the United States. He will take office at a time when serious problems are tearing our nation apart. Will the backwoods lawyer from Illinois be able to calm the hotheads on both sides?

SOUTH CAROLINA LEAVES THE UNION

COLUMBIA, SOUTH CAROLINA, DECEMBER 20, 1860 — South Carolina has announced that it is seceding, or withdrawing, from the Union. Other states are expected to follow soon. The Southern states have said that if Lincoln were elected President they would no longer remain part of the United States.

SOUTHERN STATES FORM NEW GOVERNMENT

MONTGOMERY, ALABAMA, FEBRUARY 4, 1861 — Representatives from the states that left the Union met today to form a new government. They wrote a new constitution that protects slavery throughout the South. They elected Jefferson Davis president of the Confederate States of America.

We now have two countries and two presidents. People on both sides are questioning how this will end.

FORT SUMTER SURRENDERS

CHARLESTOWN, SOUTH CAROLINA, APRIL 13, 1861 — This morning the Confederate flag flies over the walls of Fort Sumter, destroyed in an attack that began just before dawn. Fort Sumter, until yesterday a United States military post in the harbor of this city, had been under the command of Major Robert Anderson. Just before the battle, Anderson had about 70 soldiers and enough food to last about 6 weeks. When confederate leaders asked Anderson to surrender, he refused and the battle began. Despite heavy fire from both sides, no one was killed in the battle. Major Anderson and his men have been allowed to leave and are on their way back to New York. Charlestown rejoices at the victory. *War has begun!*

Fabulous Firsts

- 1858: A pencil with an eraser, the first of its kind, was patented by H. L. Lipman of Philadelphia.

- OCTOBER 1861: The Pony Express service closed down after eighteen months. In that short time, it carried 34,753 pieces of mail, losing only one mail sack. The first Pony Express rider left St. Joseph, Missouri, in April 1860. It took eleven days for that mail to reach Sacramento, California. The charge was $5.00 to send a half ounce of mail.

LINCOLN FEARS FOR GOVERNMENT'S SAFETY

APRIL 15, 1861 — President Lincoln called today for 75,000 volunteers to save the capital from attack. The Seventh Regiment, New York State Militia, will leave its headquarters in New York City to protect the government in Washington City.

CHEERS FOR THE SEVENTH

NEW YORK CITY, APRIL 23, 1861 — It is four days since the Seventh Regiment left New York City. In Maryland, they encountered angry mobs. Rebels sympathetic to the South have torn up the railroad tracks and sabotaged the bridges. The determined Seventh worked through the night to replace the rails.

Meanwhile, President Lincoln is reported suffering from nervous tension. *The Capitol, he says, must be protected at all costs.*

APRIL 26, 1861 — Around noon on the 25th a mighty shout was heard. A long line of railroad cars filled with soldiers of the Seventh Regiment finally reached the capital. The tired, dusty soldiers brushed off their uniforms and marched in splendid style toward the White House. Abraham Lincoln was said to be the happiest man in town. Mrs. Lincoln presented the regiment with a bouquet of flowers. The entire city danced with delight at the sight of the mighty Seventh.

Here is a poem recognizing the Seventh's role in restoring the track and saving the capital.

> Plod! plod! plod! plod!
> Over gravel, over sod
> Over up-torn railroad tracks,
> With their bending, belted backs,
> *Marched the Seventh!*

What Will They Think of Next?

- At baseball games, fans are now standing up and stretching just before the home team comes to bat in the seventh inning. Will this new seventh-inning stretch catch on?

- Inventor and balloonist Thaddeus Lowe was appointed by President Lincoln as commander of the newly formed Army Balloon Corps.

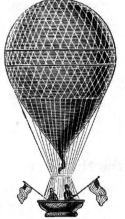

Skates

The American Parlor or Floor Skate, Hard Rubber Rollers, Antifriction Axles

Also, 50,000 pair of Ladies' and Gents' Ice Skates, made from welded steel and iron hardened; Skate straps and Leather goods of every description; Fogg's improved Lever Skate Buckle. Sole Agent for celebrated Skates.

FREDERICK STEVENS • 215 Pearl Street, New York

◆►CLASSIFIED ADS

Marbles: the popular after-school sport

THE PICTURE TELLS A STORY
*Departure of the Seventh Regiment
for the War, April 19, 1861*

DIMENSIONS: **66 in. x 96 in.**　　MEDIUM: **oil on canvas**　　DATE: **1869**

ABOUT THE ARTIST: *Thomas Nast*

Although he was born in Germany in 1840, Thomas Nast became one of the leading illustrators and cartoonists in the United States. Nast was assigned by the magazine *Harper's Weekly* to sketch the Seventh Regiment marching down Broadway. Nine years later, he made this large oil painting of the scene. Nast's paintings and illustrations of the drama of the Civil War were so exciting that President Lincoln called him "my best recruiting sergeant."

✪ *Questions for Class Discussion*

1 Why is The Seventh Regiment parading?

They are the first militia regiment asked to defend the capital. They are en route to Washington City after the Confederate rebels fired at Fort Sumter, South Carolina.

2 How does the painting show the excitement of the moment?

Everything seems to be moving—applauding civilians, marching men, densely packed spectators. Children climb to the top of lampposts to get a better view. The onlookers do not want to miss what may turn out to be the greatest event of their lives.

3 What was New York's favorite patriotic decoration?

New York's favorite patriotic decoration was the flag as is evidenced in the many flags we see here hanging from windows and balconies. A report in the *New York Times* stated that "the Stars and Stripes were everywhere."

4 **What sounds would you have heard at the parade?**

The noise was reported to be deafening. You might have heard the trampling of the soldiers' boots on the cobblestone streets, the cheers of the crowds hanging from windows or perched on rooftops, the cries of the newspaper boys—"Seventh Regiment leaves to defend Washington"—and the roll of the drum and the marching beat of bands (even though they are not visible in this painted scene).

5 **Major Robert Anderson, the officer who surrendered Fort Sumter to the Confederates, is standing on the balcony at the left of this painting. How do you think the Union soldiers reacted to him?**

New York welcomed Major Robert Anderson as the first hero of the Civil War. As each company of the Seventh Regiment passed before him, the men stopped, took off their caps, and cheered with all their might.

6 **Is this the re-creation of an actual event?**

The route that the departing Seventh Regiment took out of New York is documented in the newspapers of the time. This particular scene took place at the corner of Prince Street and Broadway in lower Manhattan. The Ball and Black building on the left still stands.

7 **What is the policeman in the lower right corner of the painting doing?**

He appears to be trying to keep order. The crowds were so dense that police had difficulty opening up enough space to allow the marching soldiers to get through.

8 **Describe the soldier with his back to us in the lower right of the painting.**

He is positioned between a young child on one side and his wife on the other. He appears to be saying good-bye. He is dressed according to orders that had just come down from headquarters of the Seventh Regiment: "This regiment will assemble in full fatigue and overcoat, with knapsack, to embark for Washington City. The men will each take one blanket, to be rolled on top of the knapsack, and suitable underclothing. The men will provide themselves with one day's rations."

9 **What do the women holding handkerchiefs at the left of the painting tell us?**

Although this is a scene of cheering crowds, the women are a reminder that their fathers, husbands, and brothers are going off to war. They fear that some of their loved ones may never return.

Chadsworth Ellis III Speaks

This morning when I passed the Seventh Armory, there was still a long line of lads waiting to be sworn into the Regiment. Everybody I know wants to support the Stars and Stripes and save the Union. The Seventh Regiment is overwhelmed with applications, and it is just about all filled up. Those of us, like me, who are already accepted, are the envy of their friends.

Everyone in New York knows about the Seventh Regiment, New York State Militia. It is made up of the "best" families in New York. About once a month the militia meets. The men parade around in their fancy uniforms. They defend the entire city of New York if there is trouble.

As your probably know, the Sunday papers printed the news of the surrender of Fort Sumter. President Lincoln fears the rebels will make a desperate attempt to seize Washington. But, the Seventh, my Regiment, will save them. Can you believe it? I will deliver Lincoln, and Mrs. Lincoln too, from the clutches of the rebels.

By the time the war is over—I guess in a month or two—the adventures of Private Ellis will be on everyone's lips. In the meantime, look for me. I will be the tall, skinny soldier marching proudly down Broadway tomorrow singing "Yankee Doodle" and "Hail! Columbia."

Discussion Question   **Chadsworth Ellis's optimism about a short and glorious war was shared by many of his fellow soldiers. How did his expectation differ from the reality of the Civil War?**

Name_____ Date _____

Reading a Map

The map on this page is coded to give information about individual states as the Civil War began in 1860. Study the map, especially the key, and write your answers to the following questions on a separate piece of paper.

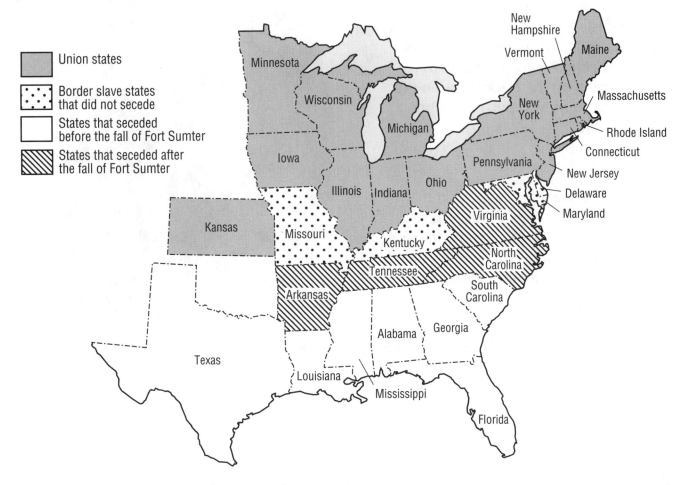

Key:
- Union states
- Border slave states that did not secede
- States that seceded before the fall of Fort Sumter
- States that seceded after the fall of Fort Sumter

1. How many states were slave states? Name them.

2. How many states, in addition to California and Oregon that are not shown here, were free states? Name them.

3. Which states seceded, or withdrew, from the United States before the fall of Fort Sumter in South Carolina?

4. Which states seceded from the United States after the fall of Fort Sumter in South Carolina?

5. Name the four border slave states that did not formally secede from the Union. (Three of these states sent soldiers to both the Confederate side and the Union side.)

⭐ **BONUS:** Which states did not yet exist in 1860? Name as many as you can.

Political Cartoons: Pictures with Punch

Corbis

Ever since the Revolutionary War, American cartoonists have used their art to make statements about politics, the environment, or social problems. The cartoon on this page depicting President Lincoln as a worker mending the crack between the North and South was published during the Civil War.

In the box below, draw a cartoon that expresses your feelings about a current problem in your school, community, or country. Provide a title for your cartoon to make sure that your audience understands your point.

⭐ Symbols

Tell students that Thomas Nast, the artist who painted *Departure of the Seventh Regiment for the War,* was also famous for being the cartoonist who invented the Democratic donkey and the Republican elephant. Invite students to create some symbols for their class, club, or school. You may want to start with a class discussion of what makes a symbol effective.

⭐ Campaign Poster

On the right is a poster of Abraham Lincoln and his vice presidential candidate, Andrew Johnson. The year was 1864, and Lincoln was running for his second term. Because the Civil War was still being fought, Lincoln made no campaign speeches. Instead, posters such as this one reminded people to vote for him. Ask students to pretend that they are running for office. Have them design campaign posters like the one shown here to convince fellow students to elect them.

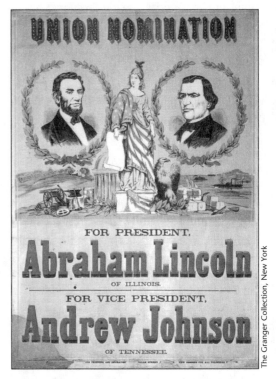

The Granger Collection, New York

⭐ Civil War Hall of Fame

The Civil War produced many exciting and colorful heroes and heroines—and some villains too. Have each student research one of the individuals from the list below for inclusion in a class Civil War Hall of Fame. Invite students to choose the medium in which to present this biographical information. Some may choose to write brief biographies, while others may choose to create a diorama or a biographical time line.

Daniel Webster	David G. Farragut	Sojourner Truth	P. G. T. Beauregard
Jubal A. Early	Winslow Homer	Horace Greeley	Harriet Beecher Stowe
John Brown	Wm. F. Sherman	Jefferson Davis	Ambrose E. Burnside
Currier & Ives	Stephen Douglas	Robert E. Lee	Oliver Wendell Holmes
Allan Pinkerton	William H. Seward	Walt Whitman	Judah P. Benjamin
John Booth	George A. Custer	Clara Barton	Ulysses S. Grant
Mathew Brady	Wm. C. Quantrill	J. E. B. Stuart	Benjamin F. Butler

⭐ Changing Times

Between 1865 and 1870, the 13th, 14th, and 15th Amendments were added to the Constitution of the United States. Review these three amendments with the class and discuss the reasons they were added to the Constitution. What effect did these amendments have on life in America?

★ USA YESTERDAY ★

Across the Continent. "Westward the Course of the Empire Takes Its Way"

GOLD!

SAN FRANCISCO, SEPTEMBER 1849 — The gold rush has changed America forever. News of the discovery of gold at Sutter's Mill in California has spread to every state.

Tens of thousands of adventurous young men have left their homes and jobs and set out to strike it rich in the gold fields. Each man is convinced that after a few weeks of digging he will be the one to discover a fortune.

They have come by land and by sea. Most gold seekers were unprepared for the journey and had no idea of the rough life waiting for them. While a few will get rich, the sad truth is that most will return to their homes as poor as they came. But they will have wonderful stories to tell of their adventures as forty-niners.

A Popular Gold Rush Song

Gold out there, and everywhere
And everybody is a millionaire.
You'll get rich quick by takin' up a pick,
And diggin' up a chunk as big as a brick.

How to Pan for Gold

1. Get one pan, either wood or metal. Even a frying pan will do.
2. Shovel soil into the pan. Remove pebbles.
3. Add water.
4. Hold the pan at a slant and twirl it about so that the lighter soil washes over the edge of the pan.
5. Repeat the swirling motion until only the heavier gold-bearing soil is left on the bottom.

GOOD LUCK!

WESTWARD, HO!

COLUMBUS, OHIO, MARCH 12, 1850 — Mr. and Mrs. Simon Coburn were the honored guests at a farewell party, Sunday. They will be leaving for the West at the end of the week. The Ladies' Guild gave Lottie Coburn a colorful Friendship Quilt. Each square was signed by a friend who wished to be remembered.

For many months, the Coburns have been making preparations for their journey. They sold their house and most of their furniture. They have purchased their own prairie schooner. It is already piled high with 200 pounds of flour, 150 pounds of bacon, and lots more food to see them through the long journey. They have also crammed pots, pans, an iron stove, furniture, a full-length mirror, and a spinning wheel into the wagon's limited space. The Coburns estimate that when the wagon is full it will probably weigh a ton. They will need eight oxen to pull this enormous load.

The couple will not travel alone. They will join up with a wagon train shortly after they leave town.

Since the top of the canvas covering looked like the sails of a ship, the wagon was called a prairie schooner.

BILLY THE KID SUSPECT IN STAGECOACH ATTACK

LITTLE ROCK, ARKANSAS, MAY 5, 1869 — The stagecoach that runs between Missouri and Arkansas was attacked by outlaws last night. The bandits got away with several bags of valuable goods including Mrs. Myra Weatherbee's diamond bracelet and a pocket watch that had been in Mr. Edward Smith's family for several generations.

The weather the night of the crime was particularly bad. It had rained for several hours, and the roads had turned to mud. Under these unfavorable conditions, the coach could travel only about five miles per hour, making it an easy target. The guard, who had been hired to ride shotgun (that is, sit in the front seat), claimed that heavy fog prevented him from seeing the outlaws approach.

Although shots were fired over the passengers' heads, we are pleased to report that no one was injured. However, Mrs. Mary August fainted from all the excitement. Upon recovering, Mrs. August commented on the good manners displayed by the youngest of the bandits. She believes the stagecoach might have been robbed by the most famous outlaw in the West—**Billy the Kid.**

REWARD $5000

Reward for the capture dead or alive
of one Wm. Wright, better known as

"BILLY THE KID"

Age, 18. Height, 5 feet, 3 inches. Weight, 125 lbs. Light hair, blue eyes, and even features. He is the leader of the worst band of desperadoes the Territory has ever had to deal with. The above reward will be paid for his capture or positive proof of his death.

JIM DALTON, Sheriff.

DEAD OR ALIVE!

all over the west they wear

LEVI STRAUSS & CO's OVERALLS COPPER RIVETED

When Levi Strauss went west selling canvas for tents, a miner told him that men really needed strong, long-wearing pants. Strauss went on to manufacture denim pants with riveted pockets.

Heroes & Villains of the Wild West

Match these famous Westerners to their daring deeds by placing the correct number in the matching blank.

1. Henry Wells and William G. Fargo
2. Jesse James
3. Geronimo
4. Brigham Young
5. Annie Oakley
6. William F. "Buffalo Bill" Cody

___ Apache leader who fought for his people
___ Mormon leader who led his people to Utah
___ founders of overland stagecoach
___ scout and hero of Wild West shows
___ sharpshooter and stage performer
___ outlaw and bank robber

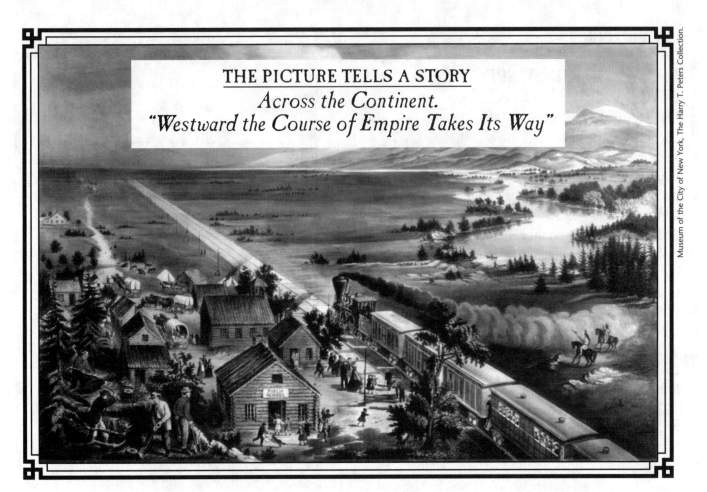

THE PICTURE TELLS A STORY
Across the Continent.
"Westward the Course of Empire Takes Its Way"

DIMENSIONS: **20 in. x 27 in.**   MEDIUM: **lithograph**   DATE: **1868**

ABOUT THE ARTISTS: *James Merritt Ives and Fanny Palmer*

This work of art is a lithographic print. Instead of making only one original version of the picture, the artists made many copies, or prints, of their original by using an inking process.

The two artists of this work are James Merritt Ives and Fanny Palmer. Ives was one half of the printing company known as Currier and Ives, which produced more than seven thousand different prints of life in America in the nineteenth century. Fanny Palmer and her family arrived in New York as penniless immigrants from England. A talented artist, Fanny quickly found work with Currier and Ives. She started there by drawing backgrounds and landscapes, often not even signing her name. For close to thirty years, this frail woman could be seen bent over the drawing table creating hundreds of charming prints that would be proudly displayed in American homes.

⍟ *Questions for Class Discussion*

1 What do you think is the most important object in this picture? Describe its position.

The most important object is the train, which is entering the town and will continue its journey along the miles of newly laid track stretching to the horizon.

2 If you were seated on the right side of the train and looked out the window, what would you see?

If you were seated on the right side of the train, you would see the natural beauty of America's mountains, prairie lands, and rivers, which extend into the distance. Closer to the train sit two Native Americans on horseback.

3 How do you think the Native Americans reacted to the train, which they called "the iron horse"?

The smoke from the train obscures the view of their tribal lands. As a herd of buffalo grazes in the background and a canoe is calmly paddled on the serene lake, they may fear that their traditional way of life is coming to a swift end. The war regalia that the Indians are wearing may illustrate their resistance to white civilization.

4 How different is the view if you look out the left side of the train?

In contrast to the pastoral landscape to the right, the scene on the left is bustling with activity. Roads have been cut, trees chopped down, and houses built. The white settlers are busy changing the landscape for their own purposes.

5 How do you know that the arrival of the train is an exciting event in this little town?

Some people are running with arms waving to meet the train. Others are waiting to greet newcomers or family members who are finally joining them. (Settlers were often isolated from their families and friends and were hungry for any news from the East.) Even a lumberman on the left has stopped work, perhaps to reflect on those he has left behind or his dreams of going farther west.

6 Look at the loggers cutting trees on the left of the print. In what ways were these workers important to the frontier?

The tracks on which trains rode were made of wood. There was always a huge demand for lumber in America. In this print, the buildings and the wagons are also made of wood.

7 In addition to the train, what other modes of transportation can you identify in the print?

The print includes two horse-drawn carts and covered wagons pulled by oxen. In fact, a wagon train seems to have just left the comforts of the town and is continuing its journey across the continent.

8 Identify the different buildings in the picture.

Most of the structures are probably houses. To the front of the picture is a roughly built one-room public school. Behind the school is a building with a bell on the roof, probably the church. These two buildings demonstrate that this settlement has planned to put down roots and stay.

9 What do you suppose is the function of the vertical poles that follow the train tracks across the prairie?

The poles hold the telegraph wires that sent messages throughout the country. At that time, the telegraph was the fastest means of long-distance communication.

10 How does this picture show the vastness of America?

The artists used a panoramic, or wide-angle view, showing enormous distances of hundreds of miles in the space of a single picture.

11 Can you read the writing on the side of the train? It says "Through Line New York to San Francisco."

This was a deliberate error. This painting was published in 1868. At that time there was no train that could travel from New York to San Francisco. It wasn't until the following year, 1869, that the Central Pacific and Union Pacific railways joined up at Promontory Point in Utah. To commemorate the occasion, the last railroad tie was hammered into the ground with a golden spike. America's railroads now extended from the Atlantic to the Pacific oceans.

12 Why would this print be published the year before the event occurred?

It was strictly a business decision by the publishers, Currier and Ives. They were usually able to anticipate what the country wanted in its popular art. After the Civil War, most Americans thought the railroads would unite the country and bring peace and prosperity to the nation. Americans were ready to take pride in their country's accomplishments. By the time the railroad was really linked, this print was already hanging proudly on walls of homes all across America.

A Lumberjack Speaks

I'll bet you've all heard tall tales about Paul Bunyan. Well, big Paul and I, we have lots of things in common. We're both lumberjacks who love to roam around this great big country. Now, I'm not saying I'm as powerful as Paul Bunyan, but I do have bulging muscles and a strong back. I'm a faller, the one who chops the trees down. Forests start to shake when they see me coming!

I get up at dawn and work until I can't see my fingers in front of my face. There's always a feeling of danger in the air when we're clearing a forest. You may wonder why I do it, but I love taking risks, and I also love moving on whenever I choose. The truth is, I hardly ever stay in one place very long.

When I'm on a job, I live in a bunkhouse with dozens of other logging men. Most folks would find the place crowded, and, of course, the talk is often rough. What you notice first are the odors. The smell of kerosene lamps mixes with the smell of drying clothes, wet boots, and a smoking wood fire. Not to mention the fact that some of the men are not too clean! I am growing tired of this place. Soon, I will pack up my gear and move westward. Like Paul Bunyan, it would give me great satisfaction to walk all the way from the East to California.

Discussion Question

Bragging and boasting were part of the Western culture. Seated around the campfire at night, settlers would tell exaggerated stories called tall tales. They told of imaginary characters such as Paul Bunyan, who chopped down an entire forest with one swing of an ax, and Pecos Bill, who rode on a twisting cyclone. Make up your own story about a pioneer or Westerner who can perform amazing acts of strength and daring. Share your tall tale with your class.

Name _____ Date _____

Across the Continent. "Westward the Course of Empire Takes Its Way."

Wheels West

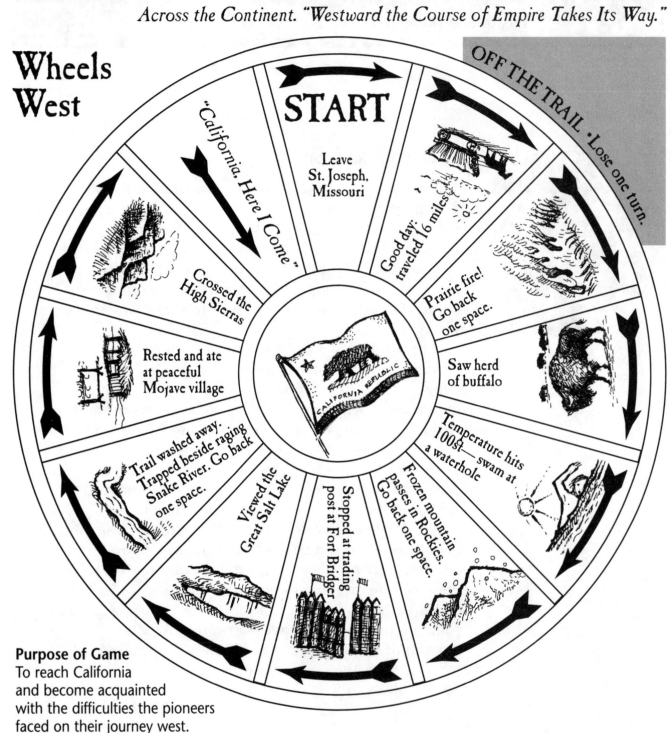

OFF THE TRAIL · Lose one turn.

START

Leave St. Joseph, Missouri

"California, Here I Come"

Crossed the High Sierras

Rested and ate at peaceful Mojave village

Trail washed away. Trapped beside raging Snake River. Go back one space.

Viewed the Great Salt Lake

Stopped at trading post at Fort Bridger

Frozen mountain passes in Rockies. Go back one space.

Temperature hits 100s!—swam at a waterhole

Saw herd of buffalo

Prairie fire! Go back one space.

Good day: traveled 16 miles

CALIFORNIA REPUBLIC

Purpose of Game
To reach California and become acquainted with the difficulties the pioneers faced on their journey west.

Number of Players 2

What You Need game board, 2 pennies

How to Play

1. Place the game board on a flat surface.
2. The first player places a penny on START. Using a flicking motion of the thumb and index finger, the player advances the coin around the wheel, one flick per turn.

- If a penny lands on a line, move it back to its starting place and flick again.
- If a penny lands outside the wheel, place the penny in the "Off the Trail" area and skip a turn. Then return the penny to the last area of play and proceed.
3. The first player to flick the coin from the "California, Here I Come" area into the California circle at the center of the board is the winner.

Name_____ Date _____

The Well-Dressed Cowboy

While it is true that a cowboy didn't need much to survive, there were some things he simply could not do without. Look at the articles of clothing described below. Then, next to them, tell why you think each item was as essential to a cowboy as a trusty horse or a comfortable saddle.

1. **Vest**
   These vests were usually made of leather and had lots of pockets.

2. **Boots**
   Most boots were handmade from leather and had lots of stitches, pointed toes, and high heels.

3.  **Spurs**
   Spurs were small spiked wheels made from steel that cowboys attached to their boots.

4.  **Scarf**
   These thin scarves were brightly colored.

5.  **Cowboy Hat**
   These hats were made of felt and had a very wide brim.

6. **Chaps**
   Chaps are heavy seatless leggings made of wool or leather.

✪ *Song Writing*

Discuss with the class how a cowboy's life was hard and often lonely and how his sense of independence and adventure was great. Then share with the class the lyrics of a cowboy song such as the following:

> All day on the prairie in a saddle I ride,
> Not even a dog, boys, to trot by my side.
> My fire I must kindle with chips gathered round,
> And boil my own coffee without being ground.
> My bread lacking leaven, I bake in a pot,
> And I sleep on the ground for want of a cot.
> I wash in a puddle and wipe on a sack,
> I carry my wardrobe along on my back.
> My ceiling's the sky, my carpet the grass,
> My music—the lowing of herds as I pass.

Invite students to share other songs of the West that they know, or have them create an original verse for the above song.

✪ *Designing Brands*

Explain to students that the term *brand,* which we use in referring to products, derives from the frontier practice of using a hot branding iron to burn a mark of ownership on cattle. The brand helped ranchers identify stray cattle and discouraged thieves. Each rancher had his or her unique design. Share with students examples of brands, such as the ones below. Then encourage students, working individually or in small groups, to create ranch names and to design corresponding brands of their own.

Rocking Horse   Flying Fish   Double "R"   2-Gallon Hat

✪ *Shopping: Compare and Contrast*

Discuss with students how the general store is mostly a thing of the past. It has been replaced by the modern supermarket and other superstores. Ask students to think about both kinds of shopping experiences and then to fill out a chart listing the pros and cons of each.

✪ *Invest in America*

Divide the class into five groups and have each represent a different nineteenth-century company building a system of transportation or communication such as railroads, telegraph, national roads, steamboats, or canals. With the help of reference books, each group should prepare a report to potential investors asking them to buy stock in their company. The report should persuade investors that the product their company is building is worthwhile and bound to grow.

ESCAPE FROM POVERTY

NEW YORK CITY, DECEMBER 1883 — News of opportunities to earn a decent living in the United States has spread to the poor hillside villages and towns of Italy, Germany, Ireland, and Scandinavia. Most people in these areas make their living from the soil. But floods, drought, and famine are very common. As times become harder, many Europeans are leaving their homes in search of work elsewhere. *Hundreds of thousands of immigrants are coming to the United States through New York City each year.*

NEW BRIDGE LINKS BOROUGHS

BROOKLYN, MAY 24, 1883 — The Brooklyn Bridge opened today. Thousands of people took part in the biggest celebration New York City has ever seen. Stores and schools throughout the city were closed. Even the President of the United States, Chester A. Arthur, attended the festivities and eagerly took the first walk across the span of the bridge.

Eighty electric lights, a brand-new invention by Thomas A. Edison, were turned on as darkness fell, and, suddenly, night became day. The amazed onlookers cheered with joy and excitement. Then fireworks burst into the air from the bridge towers.

The Brooklyn Bridge was the dream of two engineers, John Roebling, and his son, Washington. It took fourteen long years to build. More than twenty-five men lost their lives during its construction.

Corbis-Bettmann

TERROR IN RUSSIA

WASHINGTON, SEPTEMBER 1884 — It has come to our attention that a new wave of anti-Jewish violence has been spreading across czarist Russia and eastern Europe. This latest violence has increased in the last five years and has resulted in the injuring or murder of thousands of people. Informed sources believe that government officials secretly encouraged these attacks known as pogroms.

Former President Ulysses S. Grant has joined other American citizens who have been speaking out against these horrible acts.

Many Jews continue to seek safety in the United States.

Ulysses S. Grant

Fabulous Firsts in the '70s

- 1870: New York City's first subway opened. The cars were propelled by a blower that drove a blast of air through the tunnel, pushing them along "like a sailboat before the wind."

- 1876: Eight baseball teams banded together to create the National League.

- 1877: Thomas Edison, inventor of the phonograph, sang "Mary Had a Little Lamb" to his new machine, cutting the world's first record.

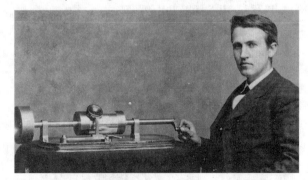

- 1878: After years of bringing their own containers to the dairy to be filled, housewives began to purchase milk already poured into glass bottles.

Everybody Is Reading... *The Adventures of Tom Sawyer*, the 1876 book by famed author Mark Twain.

MISS LIBERTY ARRIVES

NEW YORK CITY, OCTOBER 28, 1886 — New Yorkers are going wild over the Statue of Liberty, which has finally been placed in New York Harbor. This giant statue is a gift from France to the United States and celebrates the love of freedom both countries share. Despite rain and dense fog, at least one million people turned out along today's five-mile parade route leading down to the water.

The fife-and-drum corps played the French national anthem, "La Marseillaise," as well as "Yankee Doodle." Crowds cheered as students and marching bands proudly followed an old coach, which once belonged to George Washington, along the winding streets of lower Manhattan.

Next, a parade at sea sailed before the excited spectators. Foghorns, boat whistles, and guns firing from more than three hundred ships gave Miss Liberty a noisy salute. New York has never seen anything like this. Surely this day will go down in history.

Bloomers & Bicycles

In the 1850s, Mrs. Amelia Bloomer created the first practical outfit for women. Instead of the wide, long skirts of the time, she suggested a shorter skirt worn over baggy pants that narrowed at the ankle.

This fashion was laughed at because pants had always been worn by men. "Bloomers," as they were called, became a symbol of women's rights.

It wasn't until the 1880s, when bicycles became popular, that "Bloomer girls" began to be seen all over the city. The daring pants offered women safety and comfort.

STEAM ENGINES TO THE RESCUE

BROOKLYN, JUNE 13, 1887 — At about half past four o'clock today, a fire broke out in O'Malley's dry goods shop at the east end of the city. A south wind quickly wrapped the building in flames. Many more businesses and homes were threatened as the fire swept across the street.

Despair turned to joy at the sight of two steam engines pulled by galloping horses. With the pumps working full force, firefighters quickly put out the fire. For their efforts, the men were treated to a supper at McCarthy's Hotel and thanked by the mayor in a moving speech.

☙ C L A S S I F I E D   A D S

Help Wanted

Female able to use foot-powered sewing machine to work in small New York dress factory. Salary of $2 for a 58-hour week. Apply in person at The Stylish Shirtwaist Factory, 18 West 25 Street, New York City.

Situation Wanted

by a respectable woman to take in washing at her home at 204 Sterling Place, Brooklyn, New York. Walk up to third floor. I scrub hard to make your clothes clean.

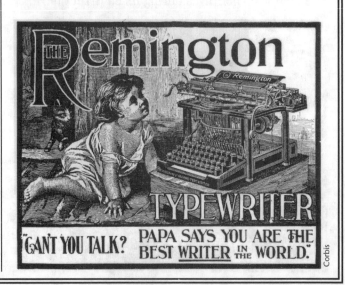

THE Remington

O Remington

TYPEWRITER

"CAN'T YOU TALK? PAPA SAYS YOU ARE THE BEST WRITER IN THE WORLD."

Corbis

THE PICTURE TELLS A STORY
Welcome to New York City

DIMENSIONS: **unknown**   MEDIUM: **engraving**   DATE: **July 2, 1887**

ABOUT THE ARTIST: *Unknown*

This picture first appeared in *Frank Leslie's Illustrated Newspaper*, begun by Frank Leslie in 1855. The artist is unknown. The newspaper, a sixteen-page weekly that sold for ten cents, was the first to show large, exciting pictures of sensational events. When Leslie died in 1880, his wife, Miriam, changed her name to Frank Leslie and continued publishing the paper, making it one of the most popular in the country.

⭐ *Questions for Class Discussion*

1 Who are the people in the picture?

They are immigrants who left their homes in Europe to come to the United States.

2 Where are they?

They are standing on the steerage deck of a steamer ship as it enters New York Harbor. Steerage is the bottom deck, where the steering mechanism of the ship is located. The steerage deck had the poorest accommodations for passengers paying the least fare. The majority of immigrants did not have enough money to travel on an upper deck in first or second class. Steerage was affordable; the price for an Atlantic crossing averaged about $40. The shipping companies made a huge profit selling steerage tickets. One ship, the U.S.S. *Abraham Lincoln,* crammed 2,300 passengers in steerage.

3 Why did these people leave their homelands to come to the United States?

They came for many different reasons. Some were trying to escape religious or political persecution. Others were farmers fleeing to America when their crops failed. Some immigrants who were desperately poor came to better themselves by working as laborers in factories or coal mines. There were also people who came to experience the adventure and excitement of a growing nation.

4 Where did these people sleep, and what did they eat on board?

The conditions in steerage were terrible. Large areas were filled with hundreds of iron bunk beds, two tiers high. Each bed had a straw mattress covered with scratchy fabric. Some ships provided horse blankets but no pillows. There was no space to hang clothes or store baggage. There was no ventilation and no disinfectant. To make matters worse, many of the passengers could not leave their bunks because of acute seasickness. The resulting smells were revolting.

Before the 1850s the immigrants had to provide their own food. If the weather was bad, or the ship was delayed, the food often ran out, and the water turned bad. Then a law was passed requiring that food, a plate, cup, knife, and fork be provided to the passengers. The food was often tasteless and sometimes moldy.

5 What is the man on the left side of the picture pointing at?

He seems to be calling attention to the Statue of Liberty. To immigrants, this statue was a powerful symbol of freedom.

6 What do the people's faces and postures tell you about their feelings as they reach their destination?

The woman in the left forefront, with her head bowed, might be praying. The couple behind her, holding hands, could be said to look hopeful. Some faces seem to capture curiosity; some, nervousness.

7 Why are some of the people in the painting well dressed?

Many immigrants wanted to enter into their new homeland wearing their best holiday clothes.

8 What did these immigrants experience when they disembarked?

They would be taken directly to Castle Garden, a circular building that was used as an immigration center. As they entered, a medical examiner would make a spot check and deny entrance to those who were obviously ill. Each passenger allowed in the country would pay a tax of fifty cents. Name, birth date, occupation, and final destination would be recorded.

As the numbers of immigrants increased, the building became too small to handle all the arrivals. As a result, a new immigration center was built on Ellis Island.

Rivkah Speaks

My name is Rivkah. I am fourteen years old. I was born in a small Russian village called Solutvina. A few weeks ago my family left Solutvina forever; we will never return. Word had reached us that violent attacks against Jews were taking place in several nearby villages. We packed in a hurry. Mother took her Sabbath candlesticks and the feather quilts, which were wedding presents. Father put his prayer books into a box, and I carried a bag of clothes. The sight of Grandma and Grandpa waving good-bye is a scene I will always hold in my memory. After days of walking and traveling on trains, we finally boarded this huge ship, which will bring us to a new life in America.

Today, we were told that we are getting closer and closer to shore. I went out to the steerage deck. It was so crowded I couldn't see anything. Some people were crying for joy; some were praying; some were too excited to do anything but point. I looked above the people's heads and saw the largest statue I had ever seen. It was a woman who stood taller than the tallest building.

Then, a wonderful thing happened. The clouds that had filled the sky all day separated, and a ray of sunshine lit up the woman's face. I felt amazing, absolute happiness, and I could not stand still. I wanted to sing and dance and say, "Thank you, thank you for letting me come to this special land." And I made a promise to the beautiful, tall lady that she would always be proud of me. I can't wait to be an American.

Discussion Question

What do you think will surprise Rivkah most about living in America?

Advice Column

The *Jewish Daily Forward* was a newspaper that had great appeal to recent immigrants from Eastern Europe. It was written in Yiddish, a language that Jews from many different countries had in common.

One of the most popular columns in the paper was called the Bintel Brief. This column gave advice and hope to generations of readers. Read the following 1907 entry from the Bintel Brief, and on the lines below (or on a separate sheet of paper), write a response to "S.," advising her on how to solve her problem.

_____

_____

_____

_____

_____

_____

_____

_____

_____

_____

_____

_____

_____

_____

_____

Worthy Editor,

Allow me a little space in your newspaper and, I beg you, give me some advice as to what to do.

There are seven people in our family—parents and five children. I am the oldest child, a fourteen-year-old girl. We have been in the country two years and my father, who is a frail man, is the only one working to support the whole family.

I go to school, where I do very well. But since times are hard now and my father earned only five dollars this week, I began to talk about giving up my studies and going to work in order to help my father as much as possible. But my mother didn't even want to hear of it. She wants me to continue my education. She even went out and spent ten dollars on winter clothes for me. But I didn't enjoy the clothes, because I think I am doing the wrong thing. Instead of bringing something into the house, my parents have to spend money on me.

I have a lot of compassion for my parents. My mother is now pregnant, but she still has to take care of the three boarders we have in the house. Mother and Father work very hard and they want to keep me in school.

I am writing to you without their knowledge, and I beg you to tell me how to act. Hoping you can advise me, I remain,

Your reader,
S.

Immigrants: Then and Now

1. Label the six continents shown on the map. If you know the continent from which your family originally came, mark it with an X.

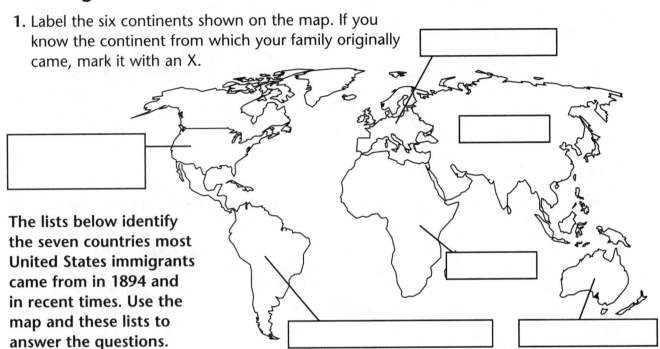

The lists below identify the seven countries most United States immigrants came from in 1894 and in recent times. Use the map and these lists to answer the questions.

1894		1990–1994	
APPROX. NUMBER OF IMMIGRANTS	**COUNTRY OF BIRTH**	**APPROX. NUMBER OF IMMIGRANTS**	**COUNTRY OF BIRTH**
1. 54,000	Germany	1. 110,000	Dominican Republic
2. 43,000	Italy	2. 66,000	Russia
3. 39,000	Russia, Finland	3. 60,000	China, Taiwan, Hong Kong
4. 38,000	Austria-Hungary	4. 33,000	Jamaica
5. 30,000	Ireland	5. 31,000	Guyana
6. 18,000	Sweden	6. 20,000	Poland
7. 18,000	England	7. 17,000	Philippines

2. In 1894, which country had the most people immigrate to the United States?

_____

3. In the 1990s, which country had the largest number of immigrants to the United States?

_____

4. From which continents did the earlier immigrants depart?

_____

5. Which continents had so few immigrants that they are not represented on either list?

_____

Statistics from U.S. Department of Interior, National Park Services, Statue of Liberty and Ellis Island Immigration Museum, and New York City Department of City Planning.

⊛ *Story Outlines*

Tell students about dime novels, the melodramatic books that were very popular in the United States in the 1880s. In many cases, the price was actually only five cents. These books took popular heroes such as Daniel Boone and Billy the Kid and made them the subject of wild, improbable adventures. Ask students to select one of their favorite heroes and outline an original, exciting, made-up adventure involving that hero. Students may enjoy designing appealing jackets for their proposed books.

⊛ *Role Playing*

Immigrants to the United States often face prejudice from Americans already here. Present students with the following hypothetical situation:

Imagine that a student comes into your class from another country. The newcomer has a way of speaking and dressing that is different from yours. Suppose one child in the class makes fun of the newcomer. What possible responses can be made by the rest of the class to teach the value of tolerance and respect for others?

After a discussion, consider asking students to role-play this scene so that awkward moments are avoided and the new student is made to feel welcome.

⊛ *Interviews*

Assign each student to interview someone who has recently arrived in the United States. As a class, students may prepare for their interviews by writing a set of questions. Examples: Why did you leave your homeland? What are your first impressions of America? What has been the biggest challenge you have faced? After students report on their interviews, work together to list common findings.

⊛ *Map Work*

Ask students to bring in a list of all the countries their families' ancestors came from. Students will have to involve their parents or other relatives in this assignment. On a world map, highlight these countries (perhaps with pushpins). Then, as a class, discuss what words, foods, and customs from those countries have become part of life in America today.

✪ *The First Thanksgiving*

Page 11, Pilgrims Pack a Snack

3 pumpkins (pompions)

5 blueberries (whortle-berries)

6 spinach (spinage)

7 stew (pottage)

4 cucumbers (cow cumber pickles)

2 cornmeal cake (johnnycake)

1 flour biscuit (hardtack)

Page 19, Feast Arithmetic

a. 10 deer, 14 turkeys, 20 ducks

b. 280 ears of corn

c. 18 (or 17.5) pints of berries

✪ *Midnight Ride of Paul Revere*

Page 26, The British Are Coming!

4. 13 miles

5. 18 miles

6. 6 miles

Page 27, Quotations

2 Abigail Adams

3 Benjamin Franklin

4 Thomas Paine

1 Nathan Hale

✪ *Washington Crossing the Delaware*

Page 34, George vs. George

Facts about George Washington

date of birth: February 22, 1732

parents: Mary Ball and Augustine Washington

family home: Mount Vernon

wife: Martha Dandridge Custis

date of marriage: January 6, 1759

children: 2 adopted, John and Mary

occupation: surveyor, general, president, landowner

hair color: reddish blond

height: 6 feet, 2 inches

weight: about 200 pounds

hobbies: collecting stamps, cards, billiards

favorite foods: crabmeat soup, eggnog, ice cream

illnesses: smallpox

dress: fashionable

greatest problem: teeth

died: December 14, 1799, at age sixty-six

✪ *The Trail of Tears*

Page 42, Map Study

a. Mississippi

b. Tennessee

c. Missouri

d. Kentucky

e. Illinois

Page 44, More Indian Names

f. Yuttahih (Utah)

d. Edah hoe (Idaho)

g. Misconsin (Wisconsin)

a. Mishigamaw (Michigan)

b. Kanza (Kansas)

c. Massadchu-es-et (Massachusetts)

e. Alakshak (Alaska)

Departure of the Seventh Regiment for the War, April, 19, 1861

Page 59, Reading a Map

1. 15 slave states: Alabama, Arkansas, Delaware, Florida, Georgia, Kentucky, Louisiana, Maryland, Mississippi, Missouri, North Carolina, South Carolina, Tennessee, Texas, Virginia

2. 17 free states: Connecticut, Illinois, Indiana, Iowa, Kansas, Maine, Massachusetts, Michigan, Minnesota, New Hampshire, New Jersey, New York, Ohio, Pennsylvania, Rhode Island, Vermont, Wisconsin

3. Alabama, Florida, Georgia, Louisiana, Mississippi, South Carolina, and Texas seceded before the fall of Fort Sumter.

4. Arkansas, North Carolina, Tennessee, and Virginia seceded after the fall of Fort Sumter.

5. Delaware, Kentucky, Maryland, and Missouri were the four border slave states.

Across the Continent, "Westward the Course of Empire Takes its Way"

Page 63, Heroes & Villains of the Wild West

3 Apache leader (Geronimo)

4 Mormon leader (Brigham Young)

1 founders of overland stagecoach (Henry Wells and William G. Fargo)

6 scout and hero of Wild West shows (William F. "Buffalo Bill" Cody)

5 sharpshooter and stage performer (Annie Oakley)

2 outlaw and bank robber (Jesse James)

Page 69, The Well-Dressed Cowboy

1. Cowboys wore vest with many pockets because it was too difficult for them to reach into their jeans pockets while on horseback.

2. The high heel gave cowboys a firm grip on the stirrup and kept them from falling off their horses. The pointed toes fit easily into any stirrup.

3. Spurs were good for urging a horse to move along.

4. These thin scarves were ideal for protecting a cowboy's neck from sunburn. A cowboy could also pull the scarf over his nose and mouth to keep dust out.

5. Cowboy hats protected their wearers from the sun and the rain. Cowboys also used their hats to carry water from rivers either for themselves or for their horses.

6. Chaps protected cowboys' legs as they rode through thick growths of grass or trees.

Welcome to New York City

Page 77, Immigrants: Then and Now

2. Germany

3. Dominican Republic

4. Europe and Asia

5. Australia and Africa